THE PEACE
PROCESS

ALSO BY BRUCE JAY FRIEDMAN

THE PEACE PROCESS

a novella and stories

BRUCE JAY FRIEDMAN

OPEN ROAD

INTEGRATED MEDIA

NEW YORK

"The Storyteller" (previously "The Story-Teller") first appeared in *The Magazine of Fantasy & Science Fiction*; "And Where She Stops . . ." in *Commentary*; "Any Number of Old Ladies" in *TSR: The Southampton Review*; "A Fan Is a Fan," "The Choice," and "The Savior" in *The Antioch Review*; and "Nightgown" in *Psychotherapy Networker*.

Copyright © 2015 by Bruce Jay Friedman

Cover design by Mauricio Díaz

978-1-5040-1173-0

Published in 2015 by Open Road Integrated Media, Inc.
345 Hudson Street
New York, NY 10014
www.openroadmedia.com

*For Molly and Mike, Peggy and
Josh, Kathy and Drew, and
Ann and Kipp*

CONTENTS

THE BIG SISTER

When my sister passed away at age eighty-five, I felt a responsibility to do some grieving, and I tried, but I did not get very far. She had been preparing to die for at least twenty years, sending me—and my wife at the time—beads and necklaces and throw rugs and old salad bowls that she no longer needed. I have a sheaf of papers telling me who to contact and what to do when "The Day" came. But when one of her daughters made the call from New Jersey, I didn't bother to take out the sheaf, since most of those mentioned in it—the lawyers, friends, and neighbors—were long gone themselves.

I didn't feel much of anything when I got the call. I thought a wave of grief would come over me at some unexpected time—while I was watching a movie, or on line at Whole Foods—but that never happened. It was as if I'd heard there was a coal strike in West Virginia. Losing her didn't seem to have anything to do with me, which is weird since Holly was my only sibling and, except for me, the last of our little family in the Bronx to go. Did I love her? Of course I loved her. She was my sister, for God's sakes. But would I give up my life for her? My last dime? What about a kidney? If she needed one, would I come through for her? Mercifully, I wasn't put to the test.

When I was born, Holly was eight years old. I'm not sure she welcomed my arrival. She insisted on naming me "Bunny."

Fortunately, my parents intervened and there was a compromise. For seventeen years, I was known as "Buddy," which was a comfortable fit. When I went off to college, I became the more grown-up "George." There is a sepia photograph somewhere of Holly wheeling me about with pride, which seems feigned. She wasn't very nice to me. I recall her being put in charge of preparing dinner for me one night, when my parents went off to the theatre. She made a picture-perfect omelet, let it cool a bit, and then threw it in my face and ran off crying. I felt awful—for her, not for me. She had a large collection of picture postcards from around the world. A few had been sent to her. I don't know how she'd gotten the others. After a few years, she became tired of the collection. I asked if I could have it. She said, "Of course not," and emptied it in the garbage. Oh, how that stung.

Though she could be cruel to me, there were times when she was protective. She learned—not from me—that a neighborhood bully had been making my life miserable. I have an image of her flying down the street to confront the boy, who was almost a man, and then a horrible flurry on the pavement—my sister in a short plaid skirt, white sneakers and bobby sox, her strong legs exposed, a flash of white panties for all the world to see. Awful for me. What if she'd been hurt? Punched in the white panties?

My eyesight wasn't good. God knows what happened on the pavement. But she got to her feet, breathing heavily. Her knees were skinned, but otherwise she was unruffled. I thanked her. She walked back to our building, a step ahead of me, muttering, "I should have killed the sonofabitch."

We lived in, or were crammed into, a small one-bedroom apartment in the East Bronx. My father, a bathrobe salesman, and my mother, who drank, shared the bedroom. Holly and I slept on cots in the living room, which were folded up and put out of sight in the daytime hours. My sister was nice-looking. Not a beauty. Not homely. Nice-looking. But she had a figure that wouldn't quit. This made the atmosphere, toward evening, close to maddening. My father read his books about great world leaders. My mother drank and complained bitterly about various injustices. And my sister, in her teens, flitted about the apartment in a little petticoat, while I gnashed my teeth and pretended not to notice her. On several occasions my father "caught me" looking at Holly and complained to my mother.

"What is the boy *doing*?" he said, exasperated.

"I never worried about that," my mother answered simply, and returned to her grievances.

The atmosphere became even more suffocating when Holly began to date in her late teens. I stayed up half the night with a major erection, hoping to catch a glimpse of her changing into her pajamas. She was discreet about this, getting undressed and preparing for bed in the bathroom, and I never quite succeeded. Only once could I claim a small victory. Long after midnight, with weary eyes, I saw her examining her breasts in what was called the "foyer." They hung a bit lower than the way I'd imagined them. Still, I was amazed that I wasn't struck blind. She was attending to a blemish on one breast, which brought down the experience a bit.

One night she returned from her date and stood above my cot, staring at me in silence while I tried to hide my erection. What could she have been thinking? What would have happened if, just once, she touched my flaming penis? Or worse (?), took it in her mouth. Would the stars have shifted in their alignment? Would I have had to be institutionalized? I might have gone on to have the satisfying sex life that I was never quite able to manage.

My bedside torture ended when Holly, at seventeen, met Steve, a garage mechanic, and quickly became engaged. Somehow it wasn't as much fun stealing glimpses of Holly in her underwear once she was properly accounted for. Steve was a bit overweight, but he was a handsome man with a winning smile. And my father assured my mother and me that people in his line of work made "good money." Still, his occupation troubled me. All that time on his back, tinkering with the underbelly of cars. And all that grease. Weren't people like Steve called "grease monkeys"? Why couldn't my sister have gotten engaged to a pre-med student? Or an engineer? I was a snobbish little sonofabitch. Still am.

Looking back, I didn't want her taken away from me at all.

Steve got drafted soon after the engagement and spent the next five years overseas, repairing army vehicles in a London motor pool. He wrote to Holly every single day. I came home from school one afternoon and caught my mother reading from a packet of Steve's letters. (In the small apartment we were always catching each other doing things.) I got angry, but there wasn't much I could do about it. She quickly stuffed the letters back into a desk drawer, acting as if she had taken them out by accident.

While Steve was away, Holly dated a whole flock of servicemen. Army, coast guard, you name it. It seemed to be in a spirit of patriotism, her way of helping the war effort. She was "doing her bit." Her visitors came across as a decent bunch except for a couple of dark, wiry sailors who were in a hurry to get to Holly. Or maybe get at her. When I opened the front door, they slipped past me and didn't even bother to say hello.

There was a lot of shuffling in the bathroom and I heard my sister say, "You promised."

For the most part Holly dated enlisted men, but there was one captain. He looked wonderful in his uniform and I was impressed by his rank. Why couldn't Holly have gotten engaged to an officer instead of a lowly PFC grease monkey? This particular fellow, I had to admit, didn't have much personality. He seemed glum and dispirited. He might as well have had a note pinned to his forehead saying: "I am now and will always be a boring person." But he was a captain.

I went off to college in Montana when I was seventeen and I lost touch with Holly, not that we were ever that close. Now and then she sent me letters, and they were unlike any I'd ever read. The handwriting itself was about half an inch away from calligraphy. And there were the perfectly formed sentences. No matter how many clauses she used, she never got lost, and brought all the clauses home to roost, so to speak. It was like having Elizabeth Bowen for a sister. Elizabeth Bowen with a great body. And that was the sister I wanted. The sister in those letters. Let's face it. If Holly weren't my sister, and all I knew about her was the letters, I would have been insanely in love with her. Forget the body. All it takes for me is a bunch of letters. One characteristic. That's my nature. So it was probably a good thing that she was my sister.

After college, I did a short stint as a grunt in Korea. I didn't see much combat, although I may have shot one guy, I'm not sure. There was a lot of fog that day. And that's when I got some of Holly's best letters. When I was freezing my ass off in Pyongyang. I heard—from my mother—that when Steve came home after the war, Holly got frightened and ran off to hide in a girlfriend's family cabin in the Berkshires. And who could blame her. She and Steve hadn't seen each other in five years. Steve, bless him, shot right off to the Berkshires to track her down. He was never a favorite of mine, but I can say "bless him" now, because I know about the terrific sixty years they had together. Terrific to a point, that is. They got married and bought a house in New Jersey, on the GI Bill. And that's where they remained, Holly safe and secure, a bridge away from a city that would have recognized who the real Holly was and all that she had going for her. A city where she could have made something of herself. Would you believe that she never went to college? (Strictly speaking, I think she put in half a semester at Hunter, and then packed it in.) I vaguely remember something about typing school. Typing, for God's sakes. I don't want to go too far with this elitist attitude. That's not me, and I'm aware that there is nothing intrinsically wrong with typing. But to have it as a *goal?* Aspiring to be a wonderful typist? My *sister?* I don't think so.

In the later years, I always told people that Holly should have been the writer in the family. The truth is, she was good, but she wasn't *that* good. All right, I'll say it. I don't think she was as good as I was. Still, she could have been a *travel* writer or done something with health and beauty, those areas that I don't care that much about, although obviously lots of people do. Or maybe she could have been some kind of editor. Could she have written a novel? I'm not the one to say.

After the service, I came home, moved back in with my parents, and got married to a woman I met on the subway—just to get out of the house. She wanted to get out of the house too, so we had that in common. My mother saw that the marriage was going nowhere. She said that if I left Gretchen and ran off to live in Paris she would pay all my expenses. (And this is the mother who was accused of smothering me.) I often wonder what would have happened if I had accepted her offer. Knowing me, I probably would have wound up living with a girl who wanted to get out of a French house.

I'd gotten interested in theatre in Korea and knocked off an absurdist play that I staged for the troops up at the DMZ line. The GIs seemed puzzled by the absurdist nature of the play, but not the Koreans. They ate it up, hooting and cackling and throwing popcorn at one another, right through to the final curtain. Without realizing it, I must have tapped into some absurdist strain in their culture. It was sheer luck, but never mind, I'll take it.

When I got back to the States, I joined a little theatre group on Hester Street, fleshed out the play, and before I knew it, I had an off-Broadway hit. One critic said he saw some Edward Albee in me; if I would just rein in the absurdist stuff a tad he'd see a lot more. He worked for a weekly in Brooklyn, but still.

I hadn't seen much of my sister at the time. One day, on an impulse, I decided to rent a limo and head out to New Jersey for Steve's fiftieth. I'd gotten a film option for the play, so was feeling flush. And maybe I just wanted to show off a little with the limo. It was an oversized stretch, the kind movie stars hire. The minute I got out there I saw it was a mistake. It stuck way out of the garage driveway and was completely out of sync with Holly's place and all the other modest little split-levels down the street. Holly had invited some neighbors over for the occasion. She introduced me by saying, "This is my gorgeous brother," which I could have done without. I had a couple of drinks and made another mistake by saying to Steve: "If you ever need anything, let me know." He didn't appreciate that. "Tell me if *you* ever need anything," he said. My tribute to him at the end of the party only made things worse. "What else could you possibly want in a brother-in-law?" I said, holding him tight against me. He's shorter than I am, so he didn't appreciate being held that way. One of my nieces approached me, the one with the MS, which fortunately seemed to be under control. "Are you sure you want to be with everyday people like us?" she wondered.

Don't think I didn't get the message and go off in the fucking stretch with a hole in my heart.

My second play was absurdist, but not quite as absurdist as the first one. Maybe that was the problem. I probably should have gone full-out absurdist. It didn't do that well. Actually, I got killed. (There were such high expectations.) I decided to get out of town for a while and lick my wounds. I ended up in Las Vegas, where I made a move into the producing end, putting together tributes to luminaries such as George Burns and Perry Como that I staged at the small hotels. There was plenty of money in the pipeline. I stayed out there for a while, but there's only so much glitter you can take so I decided to move back to Manhattan, my spiritual home. Obviously there's glitter in Manhattan, but it's authentic glitter, not the superficial kind you get in Vegas.

We lost our parents, within the same week, which brought Holly and me a little closer. My nieces were away at school, so Holly went up to the Bronx and took care of everything—I'll give her that—the cremations, the disposition of their meager possessions. At least, I thought they were meager. I know my mother had jewelry that must have been worth something. It crossed my mind that maybe Holly scooped it up—and whatever else that was lying around up there, but I never questioned her about it. If it was helpful to her, let her go crazy with it. (She did throw me my father's ring, so I guess we're even.)

With my parents gone, Holly felt a need to take over the mothering role—"Are you sure you're dressed for the weather? And you're eating properly?" This of course irritated me. I had a quick second marriage, to a Bangladeshi, which also didn't work out—the clash of cultures—so maybe Holly felt that I needed someone to look after me. I could have dealt with that if she hadn't taken on a New Jersey accent. It was so thick that I thought it might be parody, but then I realized that nope, this is it, this is your sister. *And where have you gone, Elizabeth Bowen?*

I got back into business in Manhattan, co-producing a couple of Chekhov one-acts on Rivington Street. But slowly, in a subtle way, I found myself being sidelined, squeezed out of the business. Funny how you don't realize it when it's happening. Either the business changed or I was doing things wrong. I can see why people might not want to sit through a Red Buttons retrospective. But wasn't Chekhov supposed to be money in the bank? Done tastefully, of course. Maybe if I'd set the plays in a bowling alley. My coke habit didn't help. The Vegas money went up my nose, six hundred at a time. All right, so there were some hookers in the picture. Big deal. To my huge embarrassment (and shame too, there was a lot of shame involved) I was forced to borrow eight grand from Holly to hold off the IRS. It was money that really came from Steve. Poor sonofabitch is up to his ass in grease all day and I show up and raid his bank account.

I did stay out of jail. Some money came in from my friends in Korea, who had staged my old absurdist play successfully in venues all across the peninsula. And there was some interest from Sri Lanka.

Holly took a bad fall in her bedroom where they'd neglected to put down carpeting. I don't get it. How much does a patch of carpeting cost? Did she *want* to fall on her head? She had to undergo brain surgery and it was touch and go for a while. There was some kind of recovery, although it was all she could do to get out a couple of sentences. When I leaned down to kiss her, at the hospital, she pulled back the bandage on her head to show me the long line of railroad-track stitches on her head. Part of it seemed to be saying "Look what they did to me," as if it were my fault. But there was also something lewd about the way she "revealed" the wound, as though we were back in the Bronx and she was finally letting me see her naked.

Holly was never the same—and who would be after all she had undergone? When she got back home, she called me each day to tell me about the takeout that she and Steve had ordered for dinner. "We're having filet of fish tonight." I told her it was nice that she was having filet of fish, but I didn't really enjoy that type of call. Still, it was probably all she had. Her world. Filet of fish.

She got worse and the calls that came in, by every definition, were heartbreaking. Except that they didn't break my heart. And what does *that* say about me? The content was on target. Maybe it was the wording that bothered me. It was a little pedestrian.

"I don't know what I'm supposed to be doing. I don't feel I belong on this Earth."

Did I expect the language to soar? Was I looking for *Coriolanus*? What exactly did I want from a poor sister with brain damage?

Meanwhile, back at the ranch in Manhattan, I wasn't exactly setting the world on fire. I downsized to a studio on Ludlow Street and my own health went south. I had to have not one, but—get ready for this—*both* shoulders replaced. If anyone thinks that operation (both of them) is a picnic, have them give me a call. Along the way, I'd gotten married a third time, even with the shoulders, and I'd finally gotten it right. But wouldn't you know it, Setsuko got a case of food poisoning and died in my arms at the Tropicana in Atlantic City.

You'd think the fates would lighten up for a while, but it doesn't work that way. I got the call that I more or less expected—about my sister. She had taken another fall and this time she didn't get up. Would you believe they still hadn't laid down a lousy patch of carpeting on her side of the bed?

Holly left behind a letter—beautifully composed, with the calligraphy and everything—saying she wanted to be cremated so as not to be a burden to anyone. The girls and I discussed a memorial, but somehow it never came together. Steve moved down to Lauderdale. I drop him a line once in a while.

I'm down here now in my studio on Ludlow Street. The heat is erratic and I still feel some of the pain that the new shoulders were supposed to eliminate. But I've got plenty of pills and blankets. Everything I need in the way of food or drugstore supplies is just a phone call away. I've got Social Security and, unbelievably, a couple of bucks still come in from the Koreans. So I'm doing fine. Now and then I think back to my glory days—when my first absurdist play was having its sold-out run. I felt like king of the world. My picture was in the *Voice*. The head of Loehmann's Department Store stopped me on the street and said, "Why, oh why, can't we get tickets to your play?" (All the while playfully pounding me on the chest.) Nor was I exactly the invisible man in Vegas. Eighty-five people depended on me to make a living. I got comped at half the restaurants on the Strip.

Maybe I didn't have it all, but I had plenty. Am I afraid of dying? Not with the life I led.

And then there's my poor sister. I'll grant that she did have Steve and the house and the sixty-year marriage, and somehow they'd come up with a summer place in Maine. From the look of it, I don't think they had a bad day together. One of the girls, the one with the MS who I was crazy about, is interning at Bellevue Psychiatric. And the quiet one just got her PhD in economics at Stanford. So Holly did have all of that. But when I think of her capabilities—the letters alone, with the calligraphy and the sentence structure, the whole package—when I reflect on how far she could have gone, and the life she settled for. The *wasted* potential. To me it's not just a sad story, it's an American tragedy.

THE STORYTELLER

Slowly it came back to him. Downing was his name. Or was it Dowling? Yes, that was it. Dowling. *Alan* Dowling. Retired English teacher . . . lived in Iowa, though no connection to the famed writing workshop. (How he wished.) Widower. Awful the way it happened. So sudden. A glorious trip to Lake Como and then a fall. They'd returned from a restaurant in the Bellagio, and down some steps she went. Bloody Louboutins, something along that line, shoes (footwear?) being her one indulgence. Out went the lights for Louise, and it was as if he'd imagined her, imagined the marriage. And a good one it had been too. Twenty years. Never raised her voice. Shamed, when he raised his. Five hundred steps to go back and forth to a bloody restaurant. (In the interest of honesty, the food was awfully good. Memorable, actually, worth the five hundred steps if it had gone another way.)

He'd gotten by, muddled through for a year or two; a few screams in the night as he reached for her—*Louise, where are you?* . . . then, after an appropriate mourning period (what *was* appropriate?) looked up an old girlfriend in Oregon, who was unrecognizable at more than two hundred pounds. She'd posted a misleading photograph on the web, one in which her slender, full-breasted figure appeared to have held up nicely. They'd once gone to the edge of advanced S&M, then broken it off. He'd arrived with the thought of picking it up, brought along some clamps, a boxed set, actually. But no way he was going to attach clamps—not at two fifty. Back he went to Iowa to look after the knee. Went well for a bit, then had to have it replaced. Got "the best man" to do it. (And weren't they all "the best man"?) Some sweet dreams and Dowling never came off the table.

Before the surgery, a woman in the waiting room had told him: "Take care they don't drop you."

Her husband had been dropped a few times after they'd punched in a pair of hips. Well, they didn't drop Dowling, he'd say that for them. Who knows. Might have been better off if they had.

And now this.

He'd thought about the Next Step, of course. Gates of heaven, torments of hell. Preferred, of course, something in between, a compromise of sorts. Perhaps a favorite restaurant. A kind of hangout. Wouldn't that have been a treat. Lots of good friends who'd shuffled off before he did. A reunion of sorts. But wherever he'd actually landed (been sent?) seemed remarkably similar to the place he'd left. He'd been given a comfortable room in what might have been a town house, quite spacious with some history attached to it . . . great tapestries, brocaded rugs and some Renaissance-style paintings. He was seated at a large desk, a great oaken thing, which he guessed had been hand-carved. Though he had little appetite, a roasted chicken had been set before him on a platter, along with a joint of mutton and a flask of reddish liquid, perhaps punch. Through the window, he could see a building or two floating and a bus that seemed to be traveling upward on a vertical course. Strange—but other than that, all seemed peaceful and might have been a thoroughfare in humdrum Des Moines.

He was soon joined by a Mr. Hump, the name unfortunate

though fitting. The small and cheerful man did indeed have a hump on his back. And wasn't there a less unlovely designation for such a condition, malformation of the spine, some such term? (Not much improvement there. Might as well stay with the familiar.) Mr. Hump seated himself beside Dowling and welcomed him to wherever they were—Dowling couldn't make out the name. Something Square. Was it Grosvenor? . . . Or Grover Square? Asked him how the "trip," so to speak, had been.

"Bit bumpy," said Dowling.

"I should imagine," said Mr. Hump. "Now, let me get straight to the point. That's the way we do things here at Grosvenor Point." (Or was it Governor's Point?)

"We have no books or stories here. Not a one. No plays, either, for that matter, although I suppose we could struggle along without any of your dramatis personae."

He said this last with a sudden foul look. And then he reflected for a moment.

"Perhaps a stray line of poetry here and there . . ."

"Poetry's not my strong suit," said Dowling. "As you put it, a stray line or two, that about sums it up. Goes right through me like a sieve. In fear of poets too, for that matter. Afraid they're going to quiz me on layers of meaning in *The Waste Land*."

"I don't care," said Mr. Hump, coming to the very tip of rudeness. "You're a storyteller, am I correct?"

"Not quite. I *have* taught literature to community college students . . ."

"Same thing," said Mr. Hump, wrong, and once again, a bit more brusque than seemed to be required. "We would like, sir, to have some."

"Stories?" Dowling asked.

"Books, stories, a play if you insist. Whatever you can supply. We have nothing. I'm sure this will be second nature to you."

"I'm sure," said Dowling, who was sure, at least for the moment. If he didn't know stories, who on Earth did.

Hump reached into a giant briefcase and pulled out a dozen or so legal pads, several quilled pens, and a bottle of ink.

"Just scribble them down as you think of them. On second thought, a single good one should do the trick. Take as long as you like."

And then he added, ominously, "So long as you don't overdo it."

He grabbed his fat neck and pretended to throttle himself, blowing out his cheeks and letting a long tongue protrude. He wasn't much of an actor, but he did get his point across.

After composing himself, he took a little bow, as if expecting applause for his performance.

"I'll look in on you now and then," he said, cheerful once again, "to see how you're coming along. Twenty-three hours should do it, don't you feel?"

"Of course," said Dowling, who felt the wisest course was to agree.

He summoned up the courage to ask a question.

"May I ask if you've ever *had* books and stories?"

"No," said Mr. Hump bitterly.

"Then how have you gotten along without them?"

"Don't *ever* address me in that manner," said Hump.

What manner was that? Dowling wondered. Had he been rude? If so, he hadn't been aware of it. He was not a rude individual. Clearly he would have to deal with new rules of etiquette.

His host pointed to the flask that contained a red liquid.

"Today's drink is Campari. If it's not to your liking, I'm sure we can find another."

"Campari's fine," said Dowling, who was a beer drinker, but sensed it would be best not to rock the boat.

"Good, good," said Hump.

He surprised Dowling by pinching his cheek.

"I knew you'd be an agreeable fellow."

With that, Hump bowed, or more accurately curtsied, and made his exit.

"This is certainly an odd situation," said Dowling, thinking the obvious to himself. "Although I suppose I ought to be grateful to be in any situation at all."

He sliced off a piece of roast chicken, which was savory but disappointingly tough and difficult to chew. Reminded him that he owed his dentist a considerable sum for his bridgework.

Then he thought: Might as well get started.

Books, stories. It should have been, it <u>was</u>, right up his alley. He'd spent a good part of his life reading, generally at midnight until three in the morning. No special scheme to it. One book kicked him into another. A visitor, whose shelves were neatly organized, had once looked at Dowling's and said: "Who on God's Earth lives here?" Cookbooks side by side with *Bleak House*. (At least seven copies of it. Never could find *Bleak House*. When he couldn't put his hands on the Dickens classic, he'd send off for another.)

Dowling took a sip of Campari. Something wrong here. Didn't Campari *go* with something? Campari and soda? Or bitters? Did anyone drink straight Campari? Evidently these people did.

Time to get down to business. When it came to books,

all roads, at least for Dowling, led back to *Catcher*. *Catcher in the Rye*, though he no longer saw a need to use the full title. Reading it had been an epiphanic experience for Dowling—as it had been for so many others. It almost turned him into a writer. Almost. (Though he did give it one try.) For the most part, he remained on the sidelines, a lover of literature. Let others beat their heads against a wall. He'd pick up their leavings. Or the occasional triumphant result. That was good enough for Dowling. *Tony*, he recalled. Tony Dowling. He was Tony Dowling, and he was—had been—fifty-eight.

It had been many years since he'd read the novel. Read *Catcher*. Quite frankly, he didn't want to read it again and risk being disappointed. There was Holden Caulfield, of course, and his attitude. His youthful cynicism. He'd run away from prep school, hadn't he, and spent quite a bit of time roaming around the city (Manhattan?) encountering a hooker at one point, although she hadn't been precisely classified as such. And there was a (ten-year-old?) sister who was precious to Holden and may have redeemed him, or something along those lines. He wasn't quite sure what she had redeemed him *from*—alienation, something in that area. Nonetheless, all of it was terribly satisfying; it seemed the perfect choice to get started. But when he thought about it, there wasn't much of a "story" to it, much of a *conventional* story, with zigs and zags, structured of course, Acts One, Two, and Three, and surprises. He had the feeling that the Hump people, whoever they were, wanted more than a summary of the plot. And what exactly *was* the plot? Wasn't it all texture and nuance? Character. He could see the Hump group narrowing their eyes.

"Tell us a bloody story," he could hear one of them saying, at a gathering of some sort.

"Once upon a time, there was a boy named Holden Caulfield, who had an unusual way of looking at the world."

And where would he go from there? Wouldn't do. Annoy the hell out of them is what it would accomplish. Best to set aside *Catcher* for the moment and turn to another novel, *Huckleberry Finn*. The Twain novel had been seminal to him too . . . and obviously not just to Dowling. Of great importance to Ernest Hemingway, for example, who'd felt that all American literature sprang from the book. Although how Bellow's *Herzog*, for example, sprang from *Huckleberry Finn* was beyond Dowling. Still, this was Hemingway. Best not to muck around with the theory. Dowling recalled adoring Huck and "Nigger Jim," enjoyed them as a team. (And didn't they, incidentally, give rise to the Hollywood "buddy" movies such as *Stir Crazy*, which had teamed up a black and a white actor and had proven to be enormously successful at the box office? Why hadn't someone looked into that?) No question that *Huck Finn* was the genuine article, but just try teaching it at a seminar. Dowling did, just once, at a community college, and almost got his head handed to him. Most of those attending were minority students, and though Dowling tried to put the use of the word "nigger" in historical perspective, they just weren't buying it. Didn't *care* about historical perspective. You just don't throw around the word "nigger" every five sentences. Maybe one "nigger," and even then . . . A few punches were thrown, with Dowling crying out "For God's sakes, can we please put the word 'nigger' in historical perspective?" From then on, he dropped it from the syllabus. Why go to all that trouble when there were so many other books to choose from. *Gulliver's Travels*, as an example. If that gem didn't do the trick, what would?

How he'd loved the book when he was a boy, and the movie as well, though film hadn't come up in his discussion with Mr. Hump. (Otherwise, he'd throw *All About Eve* at him—*Double Indemnity*—don't get him started.) Dowling recalled that Gulliver was a young man of average height who found himself in a land populated by tiny people (Lilliputians?) each one no bigger than a thimble. At one point, they overpower him and tie him to the ground. Dowling could see the illustration clearly, in some children's book. Gulliver's long hair and look of puzzlement. (Or was that Lancelot?) No doubt Gulliver escaped (there were other adventures in the book—something to do with horse-like creatures), but Samuel Johnson's eighteenth-century summary kept nagging at him: *Big and little, and there you have it.*

He decided to turn to *Middlemarch*. There was a novel for you. How he'd loved it. Well, not quite *loved* it, but certainly admired it. A great battleship of a novel is what it was. All the intertwining plot lines, although he couldn't quite recall what they were. Someone was a doctor and made an awfully good case for why certain individuals turned to medicine. (Dowling would bring this up at faculty wine and cheese get-togethers.) And that was only *two pages* of a monster of a novel. And of course, there was Casaubon. What a character he was. Gloomy fellow. Disappointed in love, wasn't he? His wife going off with some other fellow? Vronsky? Was that his name? Or perhaps he was the one in *Anna Karenina*. But oh, that Casaubon. No one quite like him unless you wanted to count Anna Karenina's husband (Karenin?)—also stiff and gloomy and disappointed in love.

As long as he was doing the Russians, perhaps *Crime and Punishment* would be the safest bet—everyone loved a good crime story. But it had been so long since he'd read the novel, and wasn't it insufferably gloomy? He had a feeling the Hump people had enough gloom in their lives, so he decided to skip the nineteenth-century Russian classics. Had he stayed with them, he would eventually have had to deal with the serfs. How could he possibly keep the Hump people enthralled by a recounting of serf grievances? Serf *issues*. Hiss and throw things at him and storm out is what they'd do. *Serf grievances, indeed, when all we've asked for is a bloody good yarn.*

All of which led him, somewhat circuitously, to a great favorite, Trollope's *The Way We Live Now*. Big novels. That's what had taken him there. And the Trollope novel certainly was big. Paid by the word, wasn't he? Or was that Dickens? No matter. What a story Trollope had served up. Melmotte, the shady financier, wading into English society as a mysterious outsider, rising to the top of the social heap and eventually brought low by an embezzlement scheme involving railroad issues. Something along that line. He was Jewish too. Important to note that. Could make a neat comparison to Bernie Madoff. But did they know who Bernie Madoff *was*? The disgraced schemer lingering away in prison and waking up in the morning with that ridiculous two-hundred-year sentence staring him in the face. If that didn't get you depressed, what would? And you needed the Madoff comparison if you were going to hold the attention of the Hump people. Or at least Dowling did.

Perhaps there was another Trollope. There certainly were enough of them. The man wrote fifty novels, for God's sakes (and felt, absurdly, that he hadn't written "enough.") Yet Dowling, with all that pressure on him—couldn't put his finger on another favorite. The Barsetshire novels. Barchester novels. Amazing how he remembered even that much. It had been so many years. A trilogy, isn't that what they were, enormously pleasurable, although how Trollope managed to squeeze fun out of all that church intrigue was beyond Dowling. . . . And let's be serious. Let's say that Dowling was on to something. The church intrigue. Bishops. Could he really be expected to get his arm around it . . . around *Trollope*, and "package" him for the Hump crowd? The Hump *committee*, or whatever the group was that awaited his judgment. Not very likely. Not with the time allotted. Or even if he had lots of time, to be truthful. Best to drop Trollope for the moment.

His preoccupation with Trollope and George Eliot wasn't a complete loss. At least it brought him 'round to the Brits, who had always been his favorites. Masters of satire is what they were. Mention "British" and "satire" and Dowling was on the floor, holding his sides to keep from bursting with laughter. Dowling had so many favorites, but inevitably, *Decline and Fall* shouldered the others aside. He'd read the book twelve times—all right, make that three—and it never ceased to leave him thoroughly delighted. And heartbroken, of course. Always a little heartbreak in Waugh, concealed, but there, skimming along beneath the surface. Some preferred *Scoop* to *Decline*, and that was their privilege. But in his heart of hearts, Dowling felt they were wrong, wrong, wrong.

What exactly did happen in *Decline*? Young man is expelled from school and gets into one outrageous adventure—make that misadventure—after another, and ends up in prison, serving out a lengthy sentence. And of course, he was innocent of all the charges, which is where the satire comes in. But what exactly were all those outrageous situations in which he had innocently gotten himself entangled? There was the teaching at a boys' school that went awry. . . . Perhaps it was the pressure of Dowling's situation at the moment, but that was the only one he could think of. (Why oh why hadn't he read the book a fourth time?) To get right down to it, he didn't have much to work with. Was he supposed to tell the Hump people, the Hump *committee* to take his word for it that the book was hilarious. And ribald too. He'd forgotten a slightly ribald section toward the end. But general ribaldry was hardly a solution.

And so it went—with the clock ticking. He'd trot out his favorites—*The Ginger Man*; *The Natural*; *Candide*; *You Know Me, Al*; *Orlando*—ad infinitum, yet there was always some element standing in the way of a clear-cut story that could be used in this situation. *Catch-22*. Filled with brilliant insights, characters, but here again, what was the *story*? Yossarian, the central figure, did not want to die in the war. Beginning and end of story. Case closed.

It began to dawn on him that it was no easy matter to construct a simple, compelling gather-round-the-campfire tale. One that wasn't tricked up and had a clean narrative that had the reader/listener wondering what was going to happen next. One that would have the Hump crowd hanging on every word. Of all people, he should know what a challenge it was. Hadn't he spent the good part of a decade trying to write such a story and come up empty? Piled up seventy-five rejections is what he'd accomplished. *Characters undernourished. Plot a bit thin. Don't see anyone buying this book.* And those were the kind ones. *Give me one good reason why I should care about this sorry effort? Why not take up gardening and call it a day?*

What flagged him on, what kept him sending his poor novel, all seven hundred pages of it, to one publisher after another, was the success story of other authors who'd piled up as many as one hundred rejections until they found one brave enough to see the genius of their work. All a writer ever needs is that one who is willing to take a chance. Hadn't that been the history of *The Ginger Man* and *Zen and the Art of Motorcycle Maintenance*? Sadly enough, Dowling had never found that publisher. And after the seventy-fifth rejection he decided it was sayonara for him as a novelist.

Though he acknowledged its flaws, he still had a certain fondness for his book. It occurred to him that the Hump people, with no means of comparison, might find it appealing. The story was simple enough. Boy meets girl, falls in love; girl rejects boy, who has a difficult time of it and, after much agony, meets the girl he's fated to be with forever. Happy endings were not in vogue at the moment, but the Hump crowd had no way of knowing this. He still had four or five hours left. Why not scribble down an abbreviated version of his much-rejected book and present it to Mr. Hump? He had very little to lose. He was in enough trouble already. And he certainly was no stranger to rejection. Summoning what little energy he had kept in reserve, he set about to work. And work he did until he collapsed from exhaustion. When he awakened, Mr. Hump, with a monocle in his right eye, was poring over his pages. For the most part his expression was serious and perhaps judgmental. But now and then he let out little yips and squeals. Of delight? Or was it disapproval? Dowling had no way of knowing. As Mr. Hump neared the last pages, his features softened, like ice melting. He laughed heartily at the ending, then sighed with satisfaction.

"Well, by God you've done it, Doolittle, or whoever you are. This story of yours is a joy, a pure delight."

"It's Dowling, sir, if you don't mind."

He tried to come to terms with the first positive response he'd had in ten years.

"You don't find the story thin? The characters undernourished? The whole premise unconvincing?"

"Oh, no," said Mr. Hump, who danced a merry little jig.

Then he held Dowling by the shoulders and said: "On the contrary. It's all wonderful. I can hardly wait to put my name on it."

AND WHERE SHE STOPS . . .

Her patients adored her. One was a ninety-year-old man who continued at each session to rail against his father. Another was an exquisite fashion model who was dissatisfied with her nose after half a dozen surgeries. Did it make sense to try again? She treated a stockbroker who had amassed a fortune of $120 million, yet lived in fear of losing a dime of it. There were more referrals than she could handle. New York City was a meat grinder. Survival was difficult for young women in particular. She'd been able to help a number of them. It became a specialization. It was her own life that Dr. Anna Kovacs could not quite manage.

The issues were embarrassing; it would not be inaccurate to describe her life as the stuff of soap opera. A single woman of thirty-five, she was in love with a married man who could not get himself to leave his wife. She had difficulty with what was known in the popular magazines as her body image. Striding up to her lover one night, naked, she had made the mistake of asking him what he thought of her figure. He'd hesitated for a moment, seemed to be struggling, and finally said: "You have nice tits." And of course she had fallen apart over this, feeling he'd been dissatisfied—as she was—about the weight she had gained, and her bottom, which had begun to droop. Her Hungarian accent was another source of discomfort. Listening to her taped voice on a BBC interview, she realized that she hadn't lost as much of it as she'd thought.

Once a week, she presented this bundle of conflicts to Dr. Flaghorn, an eighty-year-old psychiatrist who lived in Maine. She had been vacationing in Bangor when she experienced a panic attack over some impending eye surgery. A friend who lived locally directed her to Flaghorn, who prescribed some medication and led her gently through the emergency. She continued to consult him—by phone, since obviously she couldn't go running up from Manhattan whenever she needed help. There was some concern about the arrangement—not seeing him, hearing only his voice—but they had given it a try and it had worked out decently.

On a Friday in November, Anna saw the last of her patients, a housewife who was tormented by gay issues. By the end of the session, the woman had decided, at least for the moment, to give in to this inclination and spend a weekend in the Berkshires with her nutritionist. Before leaving Anna's office, the patient had, for the first time, said goodbye with a hug.

Anna kicked off her shoes, lit a Gauloise, smoked it in luxury, and made her weekly call to Flaghorn. Her intention was to focus on several of her key conflicts—her tormented love life, the feeling that she was overweight and shaped like a dumpling. Irritatingly, she spent virtually the entire session berating herself for the impulsive purchase of a $2,000 pair of Jimmy Choos. Though she could feel Flaghorn's comforting presence throughout the hour, and picture the kindness of his eyes, he said little, other than to ask if she had enjoyed wearing the shoes. But that was enough to calm her. He surprised her at the end of the session by telling her he had decided to retire. She mustn't be alarmed. He would continue to check in and see how she was doing. He had in mind an excellent referral. Anna received the news with equanimity. She'd been aware of

Flaghorn's advancing age. It would be fun—if "fun" was the word—to see someone face-to-face.

No sooner had he hung up the phone than Flaghorn became aware once more of the woman in the apartment above, pacing the floor in what sounded like wooden clogs. Heavy ones. There was no point in calling her or knocking on her door. She was an old woman, older than Flaghorn. She couldn't sleep at night. The one thing she seemed able to do was pace the floor. He wondered if he would have been quite so upset if he hadn't decided to give up his practice. The plan—and they had gone ahead with it—was for Flaghorn and his wife to sell their home in Maine and to retire in Coral Gables, Florida. They'd gotten a decent price for the house, put a down payment on a condominium that was under construction in Florida— and taken temporary quarters in Bangor. In the meanwhile, Flaghorn had suffered a second heart attack and was advised not to travel until he'd made a full recovery, which was far from assured. His wife's health was frail as well. And they had not factored in the constant pacing of the woman above them in the two-family rental. There was a solution—an offer to the woman of carpeting, or perhaps another temporary rental— but Flaghorn found that he was unable to focus on a correct way to proceed. His head was flooded with dark and confusing thoughts. His age weighed heavily on him. Years of training went out the window.

The person he called, Miss Nettigan, was a social worker he'd been introduced to at the hospital. A woman in her early forties, she was slim as a whisker; her countenance was grave. Yet he was drawn to her. Not sexually, God knows, although that particular flame hadn't entirely been snuffed out. For all the slenderness of her frame—she was a marathon runner, incidentally—there was a core of strength about her, as if she were a sapling that would remain upright in a hurricane. He'd sat next to her in the hospital cafeteria and gotten to know her a bit. Her reputation in the small city had gone on ahead of her. She'd worked miracles with victims of trauma. Flaghorn did not feel that he fit into that category. Yet he decided, in what was becoming his grief, to call Miss Nettigan.

The home in which Miss Nettigan saw her patients was not much bigger than a doll's house. Unsurprisingly, it was immaculate. He had to use the bathroom and was barely able to squeeze himself upstairs on the narrow staircase. The study in which she worked was crowded in with books, limiting the living space even more. Flaghorn glanced at a few of the titles. Novels, scholarly works. He was aware of each of the books, had wanted to buy them, but had not gotten around to it. In this setting, away from the cafeteria's glare, there seemed to be a light in Miss Nettigan's eyes. He'd never met anyone who was quite so composed. Flaghorn had always been leery of the spiritual, but he felt, sitting opposite this woman, that he might have been in a cathedral. Perhaps it was time for him to change course. Hadn't his great god, Freud, kept the door open just a crack to the Next World? In a great rush, he spoke to her of his fears . . . loss, abandonment, death, of course, and blindness. Miss Nettigan came across to him as someone who had made her way through a world of fear (a valley?) and come back (been returned?) safely. She gave him a mantra: *Don't be afraid.* My God, was she insulting him, a man of science, or what passed for it? The banality of it. And yet he clung to the three words. He was comforted. He thought about hugging her. Fearing she would break in his arms, he simply thanked her and shook her hand.

Who would ever guess that Miss Nettigan, outwardly a model of composure, was a bundle of nerves. She had agreed to marry an academic who was much younger than she was. The wedding was a month off, and she was far from confident that she'd made the right decision. A film company had shot a low-budget film in the area that summer. The director had gone seriously over budget and experienced several panic attacks. He had been referred to Miss Nettigan, who had been able to calm him and to see him through the shooting, which would continue on to Vancouver. The film director was so delighted with the brief therapy—and with Miss Nettigan—that he asked her if she would like to join his company as an executive producer. Never mind that she lacked experience. He had been exposed to her "touch" and was confident that she would be a valuable addition to his group. The compensation, though it wasn't much of an issue to Miss Nettigan, was impressive.

Suddenly she had a decision to make. She loved the movies, the splashiness of the film world, which was in such direct contrast to the sobriety, the somberness of the work she did. But the change would mean giving up her practice, abandoning her patients, at least one of whom was suicidal. There would have to be a move to the West Coast, a full continent away from the town in which she was born. And of course there was the impending wedding. She could not imagine that her fiancé would countenance a move out west. Nor was she sure she would want him to come with her. She had an agonizing decision to make and did not feel she could make it on her own. One name came to mind. Selfowitz. A strange man, but by all accounts a brilliant one. Each year, he rented a huge cabin in the Maine woods and invited his patients, of all things, to spend a week with him—hunting, fishing, performing theatricals, and playing games in the forest. To cap it off, he was an Orthodox Jew. She'd been introduced to him at a community barbecue, not that an introduction was necessary—she'd read several of his books. His reputation was one of treating only major figures—film stars, ball players, titans of industry. No doubt his fees were astronomical. Yet still, she might be able to afford a consultation.

Considering his reputation—psychiatrist to the stars—the office of Selfowitz was surprisingly modest. A bit gloomy, actually. The furniture was frayed, the lighting weak, almost funereal. She wondered if he hadn't chosen the décor for effect. If so, what effect was he trying to convey? Austerity? Serious thought? She had no idea. But no sooner had she entered his office than she felt faint and had to lie down. He took her pulse and said it was a bit "patchy," which was not encouraging. But his smile was. He assured her that she would be all right, then asked about her medication. It was fairly standard, but she'd had four steaming cups of black coffee in the hours previous. Nerves, apprehension. Could she measure up to his important patients? Clearly, the caffeine was the villain. She'd had enough of it to put anyone out of sorts.

When she'd recovered to the point that she could tell her story, she presented it in a measured and quietly confident style. She had more or less rehearsed it on the train down from Bangor. Selfowitz took some notes; now and then he'd remove his skullcap, then slap it back on, as if he were carrying on a war between science—his brand of science—and religious belief. He let her go on for fifteen minutes or so, then held up a hand and stopped her. It was as if a passenger had reached over and grabbed the wheel of a car she had been driving. This was disturbing, but only momentarily.

He suggested—*told* her—it wasn't the career change that had put her in a shit storm. (That was the wording he used.) Take the job if it appealed to her. She would get used to California. Have little difficulty making new friends. The sheer adventure of it would be a tonic. Her patients would get along. There were skilled mental-health people in the area. Should the new career not work out, she would always have her own profession to fall back on.

But the young man she planned to marry was another story. An economics major, he had twice been caught plagiarizing and been thrown out of the university. He had come on to several of her girlfriends. Passing through customs in Aruba, he had, without notifying her, slipped a package of amphetamines into Miss Nettigan's suitcase. Only recently had he revealed that he'd been married twice before. Did she want to be tied to a man who had—putting the best face on it—such grave character flaws?

Miss Nettigan wasn't used to being "instructed." Yet she felt slapped awake. The style was so dramatically at variance with hers. It was as if Selfowitz had compressed twenty sessions into one. The effect was rough and cleansing. The road was clear. *California, here I come.* She took a few minutes to steady herself. Then she thanked him with a firm handshake, just as he was putting the yarmulke back on his head.

Selfowitz saw two more patients that day—a former National League MVP who was undecided about whether to retire, and the head of a bottling company who was in the middle of a bitter divorce. (Was there any other kind?)

Though he enjoyed the work, he was relieved that the week was at an end. Almost eagerly, he made out two checks for the adopted twins' tuition—one for Stanford, the other for Brown. He couldn't have been more pleased by their performance at school. Both were straight-A students. The girl was a soccer star; the boy had distinguished himself in science. His younger, biological daughter had not fared as well. More physically attractive than the others—the word "knockout" applied—she had shown promise as a poet. He'd adored her from the moment she was born, and with good reason—until she turned seventeen and went careering off in a dark direction.

She'd been ordered to leave two boarding schools, had several DUIs, and had gotten hold of his ATM card, draining $10,000 from his checking account. Selfowitz was a widower. The year she spent living with him was a disaster. Standing beneath the awning of his building, he had watched her suddenly jump on the back of a motorbike and drive off with a doorman who had just arrived from Chechnya. That was the last he'd seen of her. Somehow she had ended up alone in Cabo San Lucas, hungry, or so she claimed, and of course penniless. She had called to say that she knew of a job opportunity as a chef's assistant in Santa Monica. She needed him to send her several thousand dollars for the airfare and to help her "get started." And he would do it, of course. Hating himself all the while. He knew the rules. He'd virtually *taught* the rules. Break the bond. Cut the cord. He wasn't doing her any favors. Was being a *bad* parent, actually. But you had to see her. Know how frail she was. Be there when she had a panic attack. See her put an invisible gun to her temple. Dramatically. Convincingly. Tough love, indeed. What if he made a mistake? Turned his back on her? What then?

Selfowtiz, who had trained hundreds of young therapists in Boston, needed someone to talk to. The previous year, he had attended a convocation of mental-health practitioners at the Sheraton Hotel in Washington, DC. A handsome-looking therapist had caught his eye at a cocktail party. She was fair-haired, generously built, a woman in her early forties, he would guess. She seemed composed, entirely content to be off by herself, and to be amused, and certainly not critical, of the swirl of social activity around her. He made it his business to introduce himself and was, of course, pleased that she had read his book on biofeedback. His "seminal" work on the subject. (The description was hers.) She practiced in Manhattan; though she saw a wide variety of patients, her focus, more and more, was on family affairs. She had a lovely quality, ever so slightly flirtatious. Like a subtle perfume. Her accent was intriguing. Eastern European, he guessed. He'd considered calling her, meeting her for a drink, but had never followed through on the impulse. He had another purpose now. He could have reached out to a dozen others, the cream of the profession. But he felt he needed to speak to someone who was totally out of his orbit. The woman certainly qualified.

Alone in his office, he looked for her card. Where on Earth had he put it? Momentarily panicked, he searched around and recalled he'd tucked it away in his address book.

He found it easily enough.

DEPRESSION, ANXIETY, FAMILY AND PARENTING
DR. ANNA KOVACS, PSYD, MA, LMHC

ANY NUMBER OF LITTLE OLD LADIES

What do you think?" he asked when she had finished reading the manuscript and begun to stack the pages, crisply, neatly, as if she were a blackjack dealer handling a fresh deck of cards in Las Vegas.

"I like it," she said. "How could I *not* like it? It's some of your strongest work. But you can't possibly put it on the stage."

Despite the gravity of what she'd said, he continued to stare at the blank wall of his new study, wondering if he ought to mount the same old theatrical posters related to past victories—or try a fresh approach.

"And why is that?" he asked, still concerned about his wall but focusing at last on her response to his new play.

"For one thing, because I'm instantly recognizable."

"*Are* you now," he said, feigning surprise, returning the ball to her court.

"I know, I know," she said, "you've given me flaming red hair and a job as a museum curator—"

"And a house in Greenwich, not to speak of twin sons—"

"And a speech impediment," she said, wrapping up the list for him. "It was darling of you to go to such lengths."

She came around the desk to rumple what was left of his thinning hair and to kiss him lightly on the forehead.

"But you've included my mannerisms," she went on,

"you've got my style, my speech pattern . . . anyone who knows me, anyone who's been with me for twenty minutes will know that it's clearly and unmistakably me. And, of course, I behave disgracefully. Forgive me, my *character* behaves disgracefully. Socially, morally . . . sluttishly."

"I don't know about morally," he said. "I think she's moral in her own way."

"Yes, of course. Sluttishly moral."

"It's never bothered you before," he said, taking a new tack. "And how many other women do I know? How many women can I actually *refer* to?"

There was frustration in his voice, since he would not have minded knowing a few. And there was also an implication that she had kept him away from other women, which wasn't quite true. He had his opportunities. It was always naked fear that he would lose her.

"I don't have *mistresses*," he said, trying to keep the bitterness out of his tone. "Ever since we met I've used you as a jumping-off point for my female characters, and then gone on—successfully—to protect your privacy."

"You've never been this blatant," she said, looking out on the leafy West Village street that reminded them both of Saint-Germain. "You've had the good grace not to go on about things we do in bed. Things that *I* do in bed. But not this time. Perhaps I'm being overly sensitive, but if you don't mind, I'd rather the whole world didn't know about the yodeling when I climax, or the Girl Scout costume. I'm not just a jumping-off point in this play, I'm a landing strip as well."

"Was that yodeling?" he asked thoughtfully.

"I never thought so, but you did."

He'd lost all interest in the wall, thinking perhaps he'd keep it blank, try a minimalist look for a change.

"I can't believe that you of all people would take this position," he said. "You've always supported me, defended me, pointed out that everything I do is in a spirit of make-believe. You've quoted Faulkner to your girlfriends: '*Ode on a Grecian Urn* is worth any number of little old ladies.' And I know, I know. You don't have to tell me that I haven't written an ode to any fucking urn."

"No. I'm delighted to report that you haven't."

"Thank you. And nor did I intend to. That's not the point. The point is that when your friend Andrea came to you in tears and told you her daughter had written a memoir portraying her as an unfit mother and a hopeless drunk—what did you say?"

"I don't recall," she said, fingering the jeweled clip he'd given her for Christmas.

"How convenient, but *I* do. You said—rather theatrically— 'Darling, you've got to develop a thick skin. I've been written about for years. It's practically become my profession.' That ring a bell?"

"Not particularly. But if those were my words—which I seriously doubt—all I can say is, that was then—"

"And this is now. Excellent," he said, violating their pledge never to use sarcasm. "I wish I'd made that observation. And I suppose you want me to pull back, water it all down, fuck it up. You and your vaunted love for me, for the theatre . . . your passionate concern for the arts. All of this to protect your darling ass."

"I don't want anything of the kind," she said, coming around once again to kiss him sweetly on his forehead. "I do love you, and I enjoy the theatre and support the arts. But if you go ahead with that play, I'll leave you."

With that, she turned and walked, or rather swept, out of

the room, moving with what he felt was an admirably confident if not buoyant stride.

Oddly enough—and perhaps swinishly—his first thought, after she had left, was of his new study and the apartment they had just bought, which had soaked up virtually every penny they had saved. He couldn't very well ask *her* to leave, since obviously, he was the "offending party." Besides, pushing her out the door was not his style. His daughter, who was away at school, would shoot him if they sold the place, though she used her room only once a month, if that. So *he* would have to leave, and where on God's Earth would he go? Some one-room flat across the river in Hoboken, most likely. He'd often declared that all he ever needed was a typewriter (defiantly, he still used an old Remington) and an idea and you could put him anywhere. Still—when faced with that scenario, his bravado tended to subside.

There was his health as well. Lately, he'd been having trouble getting to the top of a breath. After a recent bike ride to the Holocaust Memorial in lower Manhattan, he'd had to walk his racer back to Prince Street.

Of course, it might have been the stiff wind.

His age weighed on him too. Though he had written of loneliness—claimed to be an expert on how to deal with it—he hadn't had much luck in actually *being* alone. He always seemed to need someone around. He was sixty-two now. What was he supposed to do—pretend he was forty-five and go to mixers for middle-aged professionals? There were actresses, of course, always one in the company who favored him—generally some bit player he didn't find especially appealing. But even an attractive actress would be a handful. He might be able to shake one loose, but he'd been down that road before—his first marriage—and had the scars to show for it.

Finally, there was his wife—and not just the scent of her and the silk of her hair, and knowing that he could turn over in the middle of the night, as he fought for breath, and hold her hand. The crazy outfits she slung together out of odds and ends that everyone thought were designer creations and wanted to copy. It was just *her* that he'd miss. In the years they'd been together—and until this recent ultimatum—never once had she passed a single judgment on his behavior. (When it came to cigars, he often wished she had.) He wasn't as crazy as some, but if he wanted to take off suddenly for Budapest, or let a fugitive hide out in the linen closet (which he'd done) or watch porno movies on Rosh Hashanah—her only concern was that he take care of himself. *Replace* her? He might as well try to dig a hole to China.

His play wasn't much. He knew in his heart it had no center. He'd slapped it together with odd scraps of experience—so as not to waste them. It might amuse an audience. But wasn't this the play he needed to get out of the way so he could begin work on something "important"? He'd met a young playwright—someone being hailed as "the new Albee"—who said he'd enjoyed his work, but wondered why he'd never taken on "The Big One."

He found this offensive and told the man to mind his own business, to worry about his own work. But he knew what the fellow meant. Why not set aside this play, remain where he was, and get started on "The Big One" straightaway?

Better than losing his wife. His daughter too, for that matter. (Though she generally sided with him, that would change when she found out what the dispute was all about.)

Better than being holed up in a one-room rat trap with forty cents in the bank, eating take-out food, fighting for his next breath, and trying to inject confidence in a ding-a-ling actress so she could face a horseshit audition for some ninth-rate production of *The Cherry Orchard.*

These were his thoughts as he put his poor play in an envelope, addressed it to his producer, then looked around his study and wondered why he could never find a stamp when he needed one.

THE MOVIE BUFF

He had a set of false teeth, which was unusual for a young man. Real choppers, they were. Other than that, he was thin, sallow-complected, a harmless-looking fellow. Your basic choirboy, or so it seemed until a background check revealed that he'd posted a blizzard of hate mail on the web. He had deep ties to virtually every racist group known to the authorities, and some they'd never heard of. The common theme was clear enough: *Kill Jews, kill Muslims, kill this one, kill that one, so long as you kill and keep us white.* Odd, since all of the people he took down—that is to say massacred—were white and innocent as the day is long. Day campers. The fair flower of what we thought of as our innocent nation. He had more guns beneath his overcoat than you would think one slender fellow could carry. It must have been awkward for him to reach for them, but he had managed it smoothly and achieved his task as if he'd been in the shooting gallery of one of our many amusement parks. When it came to capturing him—two parking lot attendants had accomplished this—the young man put up no resistance. "May I have an ice cream cone?" he'd asked, after he'd been apprehended. "One scoop of vanilla, the other chocolate." This after slaughtering seventy-five picnickers. It was a wish that would be granted, much later, at the hearing.

He was remanded, if that's the word—this is not my field— to custody in a psychiatric institute and immediately put under examination by the best of our world-renowned mental-health professionals. After forty-eight hours of intensive interviews, he was declared to be insane, incapable of knowing what he was doing. Slaughtering innocents? He might as well have been washing dishes.

I hesitate to call the hearing and the sentencing that followed a farce, though both were predictable and a waste, in my view, of our precious taxpayer dollars. Relatives of the victims turned out in great numbers. Now and then there was a forlorn cry of outrage. But for the most part, the group was numbed, knowing in advance the nature of the so-called sentence. An insanity defense is as easy to achieve in our country as getting out of a traffic ticket is in others. He was to be kept in a secure facility for a period of five years, during which time he would be studied virtually day and night by—once again— the finest minds in our psychiatric community. At the end of his confinement, if he were to be found completely free of violent tendencies . . . if the killing spree were deemed to be— as the Americans put it—a one-shot, he was to be set free to go about his business. And a grisly sort of business it might be, or so it was felt by many of us. This enlightened incarceration was, of course, thought to be an absurdity by many around the globe. It had taken root many years back when a group of our (unelected) elders concluded that there was no point to a long confinement—or a death penalty, for that matter—if the individual, the offender, could be "cured" and no longer deemed a threat to the community.

And thus, after five years and some muffled sounds of unrest at a hearing, Bernhard Asmund was set free and returned to his cabin in a remote forest area of this country of ours, one that had won awards for being the most enlightened nation on the planet. The voters were citizens of countries that still held fast to the death penalty and no doubt would have administered it to the likes of Bernhard Asmund.

I was outraged by the whole business, though I confess that, even though I am often in a boil about some senseless tragedy, I'm one of those people who never gets around to doing anything about it. I might fire off a letter to the editor of one of our presses. But then, in time, my outrage tends to taper off and disappear into a fog of helplessness. And I do nothing.

This was about to change.

Five years passed. Nothing more was heard from Bernhard Asmund. It seemed as if we had justifiably earned our kudos. (There's a word for you.) Our benign system appeared to have worked. And then Asmund was heard from again. With a vengeance. The killing field (what other phrase was suitable?) was a small church near the very cottage to which Asmund was thought to have retired. There were seventeen parishioners at the fateful service. The "reformed" Asmund took a seat in the rear of the small house of worship, listened attentively to a good part of the reverend's sermon, and then, almost as if he were bored, went about his deadly routine. The *assignment* he'd given to himself. None of the parishioners were spared. The reverend would live out his days as a quadriplegic. Asmund was found in a woodshed close to his cabin and seemed puzzled by the caution and apprehension of the police who took him into custody.

Though we have been geographically blessed—with mineral riches and a great expanse of territory—our population is sparse. It is not an exaggeration to call us a nation of cousins. Thus, it was far from astonishing that a nephew of mine was among the victims of one of Asmund's killing sprees. The second of them. I did not see much of Albert. He was a scientist who spent much of his time in a laboratory. He was probably gay, not that his orientation meant much to me. He studied some obscure tissue sampling and was likely searching for a cancer cure. And why should he do anything different? Weren't countless numbers of others doing the same? I liked him—I am a widower and have no children. But I did not love him. He had a kind of nose-in-the-air academic style that annoyed me, a way of sniffing at my work. The owner of a film distribution company, I was in "commerce." Though he never said so, this put me in some lesser category. Still, he was my only blood relative. And to have him swept away like dust by someone I consider to be . . . what? Vermin? Here is where I become choked with rage and unable to communicate effectively. Of course I'm aware that there are those who consider even the Asmunds among us to be part of the human family. As such, it is our obligation to redeem such individuals rather than to consider them worthless (vermin?) and rid ourselves of their existence.

In a sense, Asmund had made his statement. Now it was time to make ours—and it was obvious what it would be. More mental-health geniuses. These days, the very word "psychiatrist" makes me ill. (Though one did give me relief in the past.)

More tests . . . more studies . . . more compassionate confinement and an eventual return to normalcy and freedom.

Asmund laughing all the way.

I felt I had do something. Not necessarily on behalf of my poor nephew, though I had more affection for him now that he was gone. Did I feel I had to act as a "responsible citizen"? The very phrase makes me laugh. Perhaps it was the influence of the Hollywood westerns that I've imported successfully for our local theaters. At some point, a homeowner, terrorized by thugs and robber barons, rises up and says "enough." Takes up arms in the cause of justice and self-preservation. That didn't sound much like me. I wouldn't know where to find arms even if I wanted to take them up. And who would I shoot? Asmund himself? Even if this were possible, it would not have addressed the issue. What I wanted to point to—and bring down if I could—was our weak-kneed, and in some ways reprehensible, approach to outrageous criminality.

I'd had enough of sending off letters. And rather than approach some powerless local functionary, I decided to go straight to the head penal administrator. The man who actually pushes the buttons—and here I go again with my Americanisms.

I decided to call in a favor from a well-placed individual in our judiciary. The result was immediate. In virtually no time at all I had a meeting scheduled with a Dr. Lars Olson, who was the top official in the area of criminal justice, or lack thereof.

Olson occupied a modest and sparsely decorated office in our Justice Building. There were a few modernistic sculpture pieces artfully placed about the room. He was a slender, immaculately tailored individual with a slight accent, which I took to be East Asian. How he had arrived in his position was of only casual interest to me. I was prepared to dislike him, the better to sustain my outrage, but I found this to be difficult. He had a shy and gentle style and a manner that I (irritatingly) found ingratiating. There went my fury—at least for the moment. He offered me a cup of tea, which I accepted. After preparing and pouring out two cups, he took a seat opposite me and crossed his legs neatly. (I would have bet that his knees were bony.) It troubled me that he might spoil the crease in his expensive slacks. We exchanged pleasantries.

"My understanding, sir, is that you're a film producer."

"Not quite," I said. "I'm a distributor."

"Forgive me," he said. "I have no understanding of the nuances."

"We don't make as much money," I offered.

He chuckled.

"Now I understand. And before you tell me why you're here, let me ask you quickly. *Double Indemnity* or *Dial M?*"

"*Dial M for Murder?*"

"Yes."

"What about them?"

"Your preference."

A discussion of film classics seemed out of place here. It certainly wasn't the purpose of my visit. But apparently he was a movie buff. Aren't they all over the place these days?

And there was that gentle and ingratiating manner. I considered the question.

"It's a close call, but I'd have to give the edge to *Indemnity*."

And there I was, shortening the title in the nauseating style of a show-biz maven.

"The Edward G. Robinson performance," I added. "In a secondary role. That's what puts it over the top."

"I see," he said, stroking his chin as if I'd thrown some light on a hitherto puzzling matter.

"*High Noon* or *Shane?*"

My patience began to run out. Was this a talk show of some kind? Yet in spite of myself—that sweet and self-effacing manner of his—I answered his question and tacked on an explanation that was probably unnecessary.

"Both wonderful at the time. It's been years since I saw either one. Here again, I'm tempted to say *Shane*—the great Jack Palance, again in a secondary role . . . I actually do an imitation of him hyperventilating and then delivering the line 'Prove it,' but I won't bore you with it. . . ."

"No, no, please, I'd enjoy seeing it."

"Not just now," I said.

The idea of doing my Jack Palance imitation in the office of our top penal administrator—a man I hardly knew—was preposterous. I returned to his question.

"My choice, finally, would have to be *High Noon*. I should add—and this is absurd—that I've always been bothered by Alan Ladd's height . . . I'm told that in order to film his scenes, they had to stand him up on boxes."

"Boxes, you say. . . ."

He seemed to have difficulty imagining such a thing.

"Oh yes, boxes. To bring him up level with the other actors."

"I never would have guessed."

"There are many such examples," I said, unable to stop running on. "Bing Crosby, for one. Dustin Hoffman, although I think in his case they do it with camera angles. So many of them are little fellows . . . Pacino. . . . But there's no need to go into that."

"Boxes for Bing Crosby?"

"I'm afraid so."

Olson shook his head and muttered something about movie magic.

"In the case of *Shane*, there is also the problem I have with Ladd's son, who became a film producer. 'Laddie' is what he's called by individuals who want it known that he's more than a casual acquaintance."

"Fascinating," said Dr. Olson.

"I had differences with Alan Ladd Jr.—Laddie—over the

distribution here of *Star Wars*, which he produced. He didn't think I'd done a very good job of it. Obviously, this shouldn't interfere with my feelings about *Shane.* . . ."

"We're all human," said Dr. Olson.

"Yes, I suppose we are."

I could understand now Olson's ability to find some trace of humanity in the most noxious members of our criminal class.

"But I'm afraid that none of this relates to why I'm here."

"Why *are* you here?" he said, leaning forward, chin in hand, as if genuinely curious. "Perhaps you'd like to show movies to our prison guards? Our inmates?"

"No, no, that's not it at all. It's this Asmund fellow—"

"Yes. And what about him?"

"What *about* him? What about him, indeed. How can you even ask such a question?"

"I'm not sure I follow."

"Well, to begin with, the man's a monster. He should be put out of his misery, *our* misery, actually, to be correct about it, with all possible speed—"

I became aware that I wasn't making much of an effective case for the elimination of Bernhard Asmund. In advance of our meeting, I'd carefully marshaled my arguments, all of them reasonable, but such was my rage that they'd all become scrambled and distorted.

I took another try at it.

"Now, look," I said, "the man has taken from us some of our finest citizens. But even if he'd taken only one . . . what grounds are there for allowing him to continue on Earth . . . ?"

My arguments had become weaker and weaker, if indeed they were arguments. Olson studied me as if I were a strange laboratory specimen he'd never before encountered.

"Now, looky here," I said. (*Looky here? Where did that come from? Clearly I was losing it.*) "The man slaughters an entire camping ground of innocent people and what do you do? You study him as if he's a guinea pig of some kind and when you're finished, you release him to slaughter again. He takes a breath and happily obliges you. . . . And how do you react? You study him some more!"

"Your point being?" said Dr. Olson, who began to shift in his chair, his patience clearly running out.

"My point being . . . he's a dirt bag."

Obviously that wasn't the correct description at all. I'd struggled to find the perfect description of Asmund—and failed. If you executed every dirt bag in the country, you'd seriously thin out the population.

"For God's sakes," I said, and I could feel my blood pressure rising. "WHY DON'T WE JUST KILL THE FUCKER? TAKE HIM OUT AND FEED HIM TO THE WOLVES. TAR AND FEATHER THE BASTARD"—that wasn't it; much too archaic—STICK A NEEDLE IN HIS ARM AND BLOODY GET RID OF THE COCKSUCKER—"

My outburst, I could see, was not having the effect I'd intended. Instead of resonating, making a powerful case, my passion doubled back on me, causing me to become dizzy and then to faint. (I should point out that I come from a family of fainters. We are more likely to faint under pressure than the next one.) I had no idea how long I'd been unconscious. When I awakened, I was momentarily confused as to my whereabouts. My head cleared a bit and I could see that Dr. Olson was standing over me. He'd put a damp cloth over my forehead.

"Are you feeling any better?" he asked.

"Yes," I said. "I think so."

"Good . . . your pulse is a little patchy. I'd take it easy for a few days."

"I'm behind in my work."

"You can address it . . . just don't go at it too hard. Now, in reference to that other business, how many victims were there in the first episode?"

"Asmund's first attack? I'm not sure of the exact number. Seventy, maybe seventy-five?"

"And the second?"

"Seventeen. I'm sure of it. My nephew was among them."

"I'm sorry about your nephew. But seventy-five and then seventeen. I call that headway, wouldn't you say?"

"In a most twisted sense—"

"But it is headway. You could make that argument."

"You can make any argument," I said, quickly running out of energy.

"But you *could* make it."

At this point I was weak enough to faint again.

"Yes," I said, with a groan. "Stop torturing me. You can make the bloody argument."

"Then good," said Dr. Olson, ignoring my extreme discomfort. "I'm glad we've settled the question.

"Now, tell me," he said, leaning forward in his most affable manner, "Cate Blanchett or Kate Beckinsale?"

A FAN IS A FAN

When the phone rang, Max Wintermann jumped as if he'd been struck on the head from behind. These days, everything unsettled Wintermann. A car exhaust. A gust of wind. God forbid a knock at the door, although chances were the visitor was a gypsy who lived, or more correctly existed, on the floor below.

"Yes?" he answered tentatively, holding the receiver as if he'd pulled it out of a hot oven.

"Is this the voice of the celebrated Max Wintermann?"

"This is Wintermann. Regrettably, no longer celebrated."

"You are, to those who matter. This is Joseph Goebbels."

There was a hesitation, as if the name alone might not be sufficient identification.

"Reichminister of Propaganda, and editorial director of the *Volkischer Beobachter*, the last being central to the purpose of this call."

"I'm honored, Herr Goebbels, to speak to the editor of the *People's Observer*. I'm a longtime subscriber."

"I'm delighted to hear that. We make no claim to 'higher thought.' But we try to deliver an engaging mix of entertainment and a sprinkling of the political."

A sprinkling, thought Wintermann.

The rag was nine-tenths anti-Semitic screed, the other tenth gossip and cartoons, many of them grotesque depictions of the Jews. Big noses. Spittle on the lips. A leer directed at prepubescent girls. It was an engaging mix, all right. Though he made an effort to ignore the publication, he found, to his shame, that the gossip columns were irresistible; an occasional feature was amusing. No doubt he would burn in hell for this filthy pleasure, but there it was.

"Many of us on the staff are fans of yours. As a young student in Heidelberg, having just had an essay of mine criticized—unfairly, I thought—I returned to the dorm, picked up a Wintermann collection, read it, and was transported to a place I wanted to be. *This* is satire, I told myself. Not the university brand. *This* is how I will learn."

"I am, of course, flattered, Herr Goebbels."

And in a sense he meant this. It was a depressing philosophy, but he had always believed that a fan was a fan. He hated every bone in the man's body, and the ground he stood on. Yet there was no denying the Reichminister's prominence. It disgusted Wintermann that this mattered to him.

"May I share a secret with you?" asked Goebbels.

"Please."

"I have witnessed the Führer himself chuckling over one of your essays . . . one of the earlier, lighter ones, I might add."

"This is beyond my comprehension."

"I saw this with my own eyes. And I tell it to you in confidence. I trust you not to share it."

"Of course," said Wintermann.

Share it? And who was left to enjoy this "nugget"?

His mother's death, many years back, had, in a sense, spared her. His father simply disappeared. A walk along Mulackstrasse . . . a patrol car pulls alongside . . . he is asked to step in . . . then a void, as if he'd never existed. One by one, family by family, friends and acquaintances had disappeared, a number of them spirited away in vans in the dead of night. The awful siren as the vehicles sped off. His building was like a toothless crone. For the most part it was uninhabited . . . a few Poles, some junior officers . . .

His teenage daughter still lived with him. Uneasily.

"Are you being treated well, Herr Wintermann? The account we arranged at the greengrocer . . . it has worked out decently, one hopes."

"Quite so."

"And there have been no irritating interrogations? No abuse on the street? I issued a directive that you and the child needn't wear an armband."

"We have been treated fairly, Herr Goebbels."

"Has the homeschooling been effective for your daughter?"

"She's getting along nicely."

"I shouldn't wonder," said Goebbels. "With Max Wintermann as her instructor. Has she shown a penchant for creating literature?"

"That has been disappointing," said Wintermann. "She has the tools, but there is a lack of focus."

"These are troubled times. But she's young. She'll come 'round.

"And now," he said, his tone more formal, "the business at hand. The board would like you to do a satirical piece for the *Beobachter*. One with the Wintermann touch, which of course is redundant. Each time Max Wintermann puts pen to paper, the result is unique. And often memorable."

"Once again, Herr Goebbels, I'm flattered. But I'm afraid what you ask is impossible. The quality that you admire requires a particular state of mind. It's been several years since I've so much as approached a typewriter."

"The Olivetti. How well we all know it. The Fatherland is

in its debt. But forgive me, Herr Wintermann, we both know that great satire often arises out of discomfort, if not actual pain. And even if this was not the case, we've gone out of our way to make you comfortable. . . ."

"It has been much appreciated."

"Then I don't understand."

Wintermann cleared his throat. "No doubt this is delicate," he said, "but *Kristallnacht* put an end to any hopes I had—"

"I can't believe," said Goebbels, cutting him short, "that you've allowed some sophomoric incident, dreamed up by underlings, to interfere with the work of a genius. I can assure you, the offenders have been properly admonished."

"I was saddened," said Wintermann simply.

"In a way, I'm happy to hear that. You will use that grim outlook of yours as a spur to catapult you to new and greater satirical heights. I become weak when I anticipate the results."

Goebbels prepared to end the call, then stopped.

"Few know this, but as a young man I dreamed of being a writer. A Max Wintermann. I wrote eight novels, each one an unpublished failure. I stopped when it became clear that only one among millions is born with that priceless gift of yours. One that only the heavens can grant. By some fluke, I finally published a novel . . . *Winter Storm* . . . you probably know it."

Wintermann was aware of the novel, but hadn't read it. He struggled to find a way of saying this gently. Goebbels rescued him by pushing on.

"It was well received, but in my heart I know it's a pedestrian effort. To mention it in the same breath as 'a Wintermann' is blasphemous."

Wintermann felt he could hear the click of Goebbels's heels.

"Three thousand words. Monday morning. Forty-eight

hours should be sufficient. You will be paid our most generous fee."

"Forgive me, Herr Goebbels, but to put a time restriction—"

Goebbels spoke as if he hadn't heard Wintermann. "If there are any difficulties . . . If your daughter, for example, should be jostled by one of our inexperienced and, shall we say, randy young officers, please call my private number.

"Heil Hitler."

Through a dry mouth Wintermann repeated. "Heil Hitler."

"Ten o'clock sharp," said Goebbels.

Oddly enough, what rankled Wintermann most was Goebbels's claim that the publication of his (ninth) novel was "a fluke." He was perhaps the second most powerful figure in Germany. Lived there a publisher who would dare to say, "It's not quite for us"? It would not surprise Wintermann if the eight unpublished novels were suddenly "discovered" and brought out with great ceremony.

But to dwell on Goebbels's "literary" career was to be attentive to rubbish. Hypocritically, Wintermann did read—or glance at—the *Beobachter*. But to write a sentence, *two words*, for the tabloid was of course out of the question. Better ask him to piss on the graves of the forlorn army of Jews whose great number had not yet been established. It was bad enough that he had accepted "protection" for himself and his beloved daughter. A man with an ounce of courage would have told the Reichminister what he could do with his offer.

Shove it up your ass, Herr Goebbels. Then come and get me if you like. Tear off my balls. But you will not get a single word . . .

And to his daughter: *Run . . . it doesn't matter where . . . be swift . . . and never stop.*

Yet he had remained silent. Compliant.

Though it was difficult for him to be in the same room as his battered Olivetti, Wintermann did not lack for ideas. There was one thought that nagged at him, virtually calling out for his attention. It was no secret that Hitler protected a small number of Jews he found useful. A master tailor. An arms merchant. A man with great surgical skills. Wasn't Wintermann, in his way, one of the select few? A human bone Hitler had thrown to Wintermann's passionate fans.

It fascinated Wintermann that throughout the war years— and before—Hitler supported a psychiatric institute in Berlin. There were three hundred practitioners at work there, some of them Jews who had been spared. Half worked on eugenics. The others practiced conventional therapy. At root and in the overall, a psychiatrist's goal was to make a troubled patient feel more comfortable. It took little effort for Wintermann to imagine a Third Reich psychiatrist counseling a guilt-ridden Nazi official.

What is your work?

Each day I dispatch roughly five hundred Jews to a "labor camp," the equivalent of sending lambs to slaughter.

Is that your assignment?

Yes.

You do your job well?

I do.

Then I'm puzzled. What is it that troubles you?

The scene virtually satirized itself and hardly called for the touch of a master. Wintermann needed only to record, almost literally, such a session. The Wintermann of old would have tossed it off in an afternoon, nap included.

Not for a moment did he consider proceeding. The notion, for all its absurdity, required a light touch, what some had called, clumsily, a style that was "Wintermannesque." Could he still produce it? In his present state, his "touch" would be that of an elephant's hooves.

And yet Goebbels, though he hadn't quite put it this way, had suggested that the very act of making a start, even out of pain, would force him into the literary posture he sought and help him to regain his touch, which he prayed had not disappeared entirely.

Still, to entertain a nation of Jew-hating Nazis was unthinkable.

Goebbels called late at night.

"I hope I'm not interrupting your labors . . ."

"No, no, Herr Goebbels. I was preparing for bed."

"I won't offend by asking how you're coming along. Did the pope call Leonardo with such a concern? But I wanted to assure you that there will be absolutely no editorial interference in your work. No politicizing. Not a sentence will be altered. In case I hadn't made that clear. You have my word."

"I appreciate that, Herr Goebbels."

"I thought you might. Have a good night. And Heil Hitler."

Wintermann rasped out, "Heil Hitler."

A restless night was not out of the ordinary for Wintermann. But the one that followed was an ordeal. As he tried in vain to align comfortably his arthritic bones, there was a thought that nagged at him. Oddly enough, it had nothing to do with the gruesome consequences of refusing the Reichminister.

He forced himself, made an almost physical effort, to chip away at the edges and to confront the true state of his mind. And then, it was almost as if he'd wrestled a powerful adversary to the ground. *His need to publish.* That was it. *His need to be heard.* It had been several years since he'd had a word in print. The silence, the inability to share his ideas with even the most vile audience. This is what had defeated him. Some might say his silence was courageous. But with no outlet, no *forum*, no means to be heard, his life seemed pointless. He treasured his daughter. But was that a reason to exist? His long silence hastened him to the grave. Past triumphs were of no interest to him. His time on Earth seemed pointless. He yearned for a turn in the spotlight, even a final one. Only by seeing the name Max Wintermann in print, the work itself in print, would his life feel verified.

Goebbels had assured him that not a word of his would be altered. For some reason, and on this one point, he trusted the Reichminister.

The story, still unwritten, would stand alone. Untouched. The editorial matter? The cartoons that spit on the Jews? None of this was his responsibility. His story would be pure, isolated, contemptuous of its surroundings. Like an honorable man, standing upright among thieves. A stately and untouched tree in a scorched forest. No longer would he feel smothered by silence.

Sleep was out of the question. He approached the Olivetti with a familiar apprehension. He had felt it at the height of his powers. In many ways it was welcome.

The fear of making a start.

And this after a virtual lifetime of storytelling.

With trembling fingers, he tried a sentence. It was gibberish, but it was useful. The inadequacy pointed the way. He tried another, then several more. The sensation he felt was much like swimming after a long absence from the water. The stroke was there.

In short order, he surprised himself by working cleanly and effortlessly. The piece was finished in not much more than an hour. He put a hand to his chest, to make sure the exertion, mild as it had been, had not brought about a heart attack. He read his work. He was experienced enough to be his own editor. Quickly, he saw there was little need to change much of it. He felt confident that he had produced what others had called "a Wintermann."

He delivered the manuscript at the appointed hour, then stood before Goebbels, cap in hand, his head bowed slightly, while the Reichminister reviewed his efforts.

To think I have to wait anxiously for the approval of a literary pygmy.

As he turned the pages, Goebbels for the most part did not change his expression. At one point he did snicker. Wintermann could not tell if this was an expression of amusement or contempt.

When he had finished reading the manuscript, Goebbels set it aside, pushed his chair back, and kicked his short, booted legs up on his desk. Then he rubbed his eyes.

"There is something I don't understand."

"Yes, Herr Goebbels."

"I was under the impression that I had asked for 'a Wintermann.'"

"As you did, Herr Goebbels."

"I made myself clear on this point?"

"You did, indeed."

"Then why, may I ask, do you give me *this*?"

He picked up the manuscript, then slammed it down on his desk. His eyes bulged. He had spittle on his lips, much like that of the cartoon Jews that he ridiculed.

"This is not 'a Wintermann,'" he went on. "Why not call it what it is."

He picked up the manuscript again and waved it in Wintermann's face.

"Smell it. This is shit."

"It's but a draft, Herr Goebbels."

"Never mind. I defy you to show me one touch of Wintermann in these pages. One speck. A crumb."

"If the Reichminister would be so kind as to point out the inadequacies . . . they can be fixed—"

"They *cannot* be fixed."

In a moment of relative calm, Goebbels said, "As satirists, we both know that what is born disfigured remains that way.

"*All* of it upsets me," he continued, gathering heat. "It stinks in its conception, its execution . . . every phrase. To think I wanted once to sit at Max Wintermann's feet. This is an insult to me, to the *Beobachter*, to the Third Reich itself. For the Führer to see it besmirch our pages . . ."

Shuddering at the possibility, he handed some cloth material to Wintermann.

"Here. Take this."

Wintermann glanced at it.

"But these are armbands."

"One for you and one for your daughter. A car will pick you up at seven tomorrow morning."

"Where will it take us?"

"To the countryside, of course," said Goebbels, with a thin

smile. "The fresh air will do you both good. Take along only essentials.

"Guards!" he cried out.

Two uniformed Gestapo officers came running forth. Each took one of Wintermann's arms and began to lead, then to drag, him off.

The soft-spoken Wintermann could not recall the last time he had raised his voice. But now, twisting his head toward Goebbels and with the roar of a dying lion, he cried out "*VANTS*." It was one of the few Yiddish words he remembered. It meant "cockroach."

"*Vants*," Goebbels repeated to an adjutant, when the struggling Wintermann had been removed. "What does it mean?"

"Some Yid trash."

"Still, it has a nice sound to it. A military bounce. For the time being why don't you address me as such."

"Of course, Herr Goebbels . . . Herr Vants."

"I like it. *Vants. Herr Vants.* Vintage Wintermann, if you ask me."

THE FRIENDSHIP

It might have been a perfect friendship if it hadn't been for a single issue that hung between us like an overripe fruit that had never quite dropped from a tree. As so often happens, there was a woman at the center of it.

We had known each other for three decades. A slight, sandy-haired man, Jenkins was a Yeats scholar who collected rare manuscripts. He had inherited a great deal of money, and spent very little of it. Uncharacteristically, Jenkins had actually invested in the first film I directed. It was a documentary about a British scientist who spent a good part of his life trying to discredit Albert Einstein's relativity theory—only to concede that the great physicist was correct in his calculations. Much to the surprise of the producers, the venture turned a small profit. This sunny outcome led to my friendship with Jenkins.

One night, at a cocktail party in Sag Harbor, we had both been introduced to a young actress named Claudia Mills. She was tall, raven-haired, cheerful. She had the slender and leggy figure of a fashion model. Though I thought about calling her, I was lazy about doing so and never quite got around to it. There was a woman in my life who was important to me, so you could say that I was covered in that department. Still, Claudia was awfully attractive, and I thought that somehow, at some point,

I would catch up with her. But Jenkins was quick off the mark. He pursued Claudia. They began what appeared to be a serious affair. It was difficult to imagine Jenkins, with his pinched ways, in bed with a woman, much less having sex with her. He was one of those people. Yet you never knew. I could picture Claudia parading around nude in front of Jenkins while he smoked his pipe and looked on with approval. But that was as far as my imagination would take me.

Several months after that first meeting, Claudia moved to Sausalito to be with her ailing parents. Jenkins remained behind in Manhattan but stayed in touch with her. Close as ever with money, he told me that he had begun to support Claudia, making payments on a houseboat she'd rented and caring, financially, for her five-year-old son, the product of a brief marriage to a Hungarian businessman who had since removed himself from her life.

Though Jenkins and Claudia were never together during this period, they spoke on the phone each night. He sent her regular shipments of books he felt she'd enjoy. He had platonic dates with other women, young women, "wards" Jenkins called them, but remained devoted to Claudia. The absentee arrangement seemed not to trouble him.

Jenkins and I had dinner now and then. He was a good listener, and pleasant to be with until he began, insufferably, to recite heroic poetry. He would, even more annoyingly, break out now and then with his own verses, which were, justifiably, unpublished. Still, I never had to worry about my appearance when I met him, nor did I feel the need to compete with him on any level. Easy enough to compare him to a comfortable pair of slippers.

He never ordered more than a main course for dinner, considering it wasteful and unnecessary to eat a salad or dessert. When the check arrived he would scrutinize it with great care before leaving a meager tip for his share of the meal. Yet somehow he managed to turn his tightfisted style—cheapness, really—into a charming affectation. This was effective, but only for a time. On occasion, Jenkins asked me if I needed "financial support." Since my filmmaking career was spotty, I was usually low on funds. But I didn't care for the way he'd phrased the question. Had he asked me directly, "Do you need some money?" I might have taken him up on his offer. *Financial support?* Wasn't that for the "most needy" families you read about in the *Times* at Christmas? As it was, I thanked him and told him—stretching the truth— that I was doing very nicely.

I asked now and then how Claudia was getting along.

"She's having a difficult time," he said. "Her parents aren't getting any better. The boy, Rory, has had trouble adjusting at school. Her own health is frail. . . ."

In a rare show of emotion, Jenkins's voice broke.

"If I ever lost Claudia, I'd have no reason to continue living."

At one of our dinners, I mentioned that I would be in San Francisco for a month or so, scouting locations for a film venture.

"That's good news," said Jenkins. "I wonder if I might ask a favor. Claudia is stuck in with her parents and is very lonely. It would mean a great deal to me if you could find time to take her to dinner.

"I'll pay for the meal, of course," said my friend who, several years before, had told me he was worth $125 million. Carefully invested, it would have grown to twice the amount.

"I can't get away myself," he added, although he didn't specify why.

I said I would be happy to help out. Soon after I arrived in San Francisco, I checked into the Clift Hotel and called Claudia, who seemed pleased to hear from me. Jenkins had told her I'd be in touch.

"It's impossible to find the houseboat if you're not familiar with the area," she said. "Why don't I pick you up at your hotel?"

We never made it out of the hotel room. When I reconstruct the episode, I remember Claudia arriving at the appointed time, wearing a flowered miniskirt, looking tanned and leggy, brimming over with Californian health and good fortune. A flash of blinding-white panties. I ordered drinks, we had a brief innocuous conversation dealing with life in the Bay Area—and then she flew at me in the style of love-starved women in pulp novels that were set in the tropics. Or so I recalled it. In actuality, I may have met her halfway. I'd had an earlier opportunity to be with Claudia—when Jenkins and I first met her—and I'd let it slip away. I felt that in a sense, we'd had a "date" that I hadn't kept. There was no question that she was attractive, but there was also a need on my part to "balance the books." The idea that she was Jenkins's girl was never an issue. Hadn't we all met on the same night? Jenkins had conveniently forgotten that. He had simply acted with greater speed than I had. That was his style in the financial markets as well.

My film work kept me in California for several months, which was not unpleasant. Claudia and I began an on-and-off affair. I was feeling morose about an unpleasant divorce, guilty about not seeing my two daughters half enough. Claudia was unendingly cheerful, almost desperately so. We got along decently in bed, though her preference was clearly for oral sex. She found the other "difficult." This was a satisfactory arrangement—to a point.

On one occasion, I was lying back on the plump pillows of her cheerfully appointed bed when Jenkins called. He and Claudia chatted amiably for a bit, although I sensed the conversation was understandably a bit more constrained than if I hadn't been there. You would think I might have experienced shame—or some illicit thrill—about the call, but I felt nothing in particular. I certainly didn't want Jenkins—in fantasy terms—sharing a bed with us. And I kept reminding myself that the three of us had met at the same time. He was my friend and he was supporting Claudia, but they were never together. And he had made it easy for us to start an affair. Hadn't he virtually thrown us together? He knew—or should have known—how I am around women. How any man would be around a willing and hungry Claudia. A shrink might have deduced that he had choreographed the affair. To carry it a bit further—if he couldn't manage it in bed with her, why not send me in as a surrogate?

This was an affair, incidentally, that meant little to me. There was the constricted sex. And no matter how hard I fought against it, I felt deeply saddened by my divorce. The more solemn I became about it, the more Claudia pressured me.

"You can't go on feeling this way," she said.

"It's something I have to go through. I can't help it."

"You have to stop," she said, virtually stamping her foot, which of course, made me feel even more awful.

If she had given me some room to breathe, it might have worked out differently. As it was, I gradually eased out of the affair. My work was completed in San Francisco. Claudia seemed to have no means of support other than the money she received from Jenkins. To salve my conscience, as I drew away from her, I introduced Claudia to a gifted Czech filmmaker who was in need of a researcher. There was no questioning her intelligence and her cheerful outlook.

"She's good company," he said to me, many months later. Then he added morosely, "But all she gives is blowjobs."

A mistake I made, one I couldn't resist, was to use the mechanics of our story—that of me and Jenkins and Claudia—as the subplot of a film I was shooting. I did my best to disguise all three principals. I cast Jenkins's character as the heavily accented German owner of a hunting lodge in Kenya. I made myself a Turk and Claudia a visiting anthropologist. Jenkins came to see a screening of the film and recognized himself immediately. (He always seemed ready to doze off. It was easy to underestimate his intelligence. His brilliance, really.) Still, he said nothing about the triangular affair, which was all there on the screen. A remark Jenkins made about me to a mutual friend got back to me: "Derek is a fine man and an excellent friend—except when it comes to women."

Jenkins never once asked about my visit to California or even hinted that he knew of the affair. But it was always floating about on the edges of our friendship. When Claudia's name came up, he would take on a quizzical, almost smirking, look, indicating that he knew more than he let on, although I may have been mistaken about that. On several occasions, after I'd drunk a few Gibsons at one of our dinners, I came close to admitting to the affair. I had a feeling that it wouldn't have affected our friendship that dramatically. But I found the strength to hold back.

It's possible Jenkins may have tried to punish me indirectly. On one occasion, he passed along a stock tip he had been given by his broker. I invested $20,000 in the Midwestern furniture company and lost most of it within a week. He later admitted that he hadn't personally taken his broker's advice, which of course was upsetting to me, though I didn't admit to him how costly the setback had been. He generally ended each of our dinners by telling me, in painful and unnecessary detail, of meetings he'd had with a battery of financial handlers over how best to allocate his various assets.

After a decade of leading a single life, I'd gotten married to a pretty young psychologist. In an odd coincidence, Jenkins and I had both been introduced to Rachel at a gallery exhibition in the West Village. This time I moved more quickly than Jenkins did. I got to take her back to her flat that night in a taxi.

Jenkins called the following day.

"That wonderful girl we were talking to last night. I didn't get her name."

"It's Rachel. And I'm going to marry her."

Though we lived separately, Rachel and I saw each other each night for several months; then we decided to pool our resources and buy a cottage in the Catskills, an hour and twenty minutes' drive from Manhattan. Though my directing career had faded, I was able to piece together a living as a set designer on small-budget films and as a location scout on others. Rachel took a job as a counselor at a local high school. On one occasion, I was stuck in Chicago at a time when Rachel needed to be hospitalized for some minor surgery. Jenkins agreed to travel up to the mountains and see to it that she got home safely after the procedure. Tight as he was with money, he could be generous with his time. He helped me out as well when I was traveling and unable to show up for an early-morning course I taught in filmmaking at the New School. Two other friends turned me down without apology.

Jenkins said he'd be happy to fill in for me. From all reports, he was a hit with the students.

Every few weeks I would drive to Manhattan to have dinner with Jenkins. Inevitably, Claudia's name came up. She was always "about to visit," but had to cancel at the last minute. Her parents had passed away, but there was a favorite aunt who had virtually raised Claudia and was now ill and needed to be cared for. On another occasion, Claudia had planned to vacation in Vancouver with Jenkins and had actually purchased her airline ticket. But she had sprained her ankle at the terminal. A doctor explained that the injury, in some ways, was worse than a break. It would take some time for her to recuperate. He advised her not to travel. Many months later, when the sprain had healed, there had been a mysterious gas leak on the houseboat. It would take time to locate the leak and then to repair it. I once asked Jenkins why he wouldn't fly out to visit Claudia. He was vague in his response, mumbling something to the effect that it wouldn't be a good idea.

And then one day—and here I have to use the word "miraculously"—Claudia did come east to visit Jenkins. After a day in Manhattan at his apartment, they paid us a visit in the country. Claudia looked spry and fresh and lively. They presented Rachel with flowers and me with a set of expensive hair and clothing brushes I use to this day. I had a strong feeling that the gifts were Claudia's idea. She made a fuss over our house and fell in love with our Norfolk terriers. The pipe-smoking Jenkins looked on with pride as she sprawled out on the lawn and played with the dogs. He might have been the parent of a child who was performing well at a school activity.

Rachel showed them to a second-floor study that served as a guest room. As Claudia unpacked, Jenkins took me aside. He was near tears.

"I can't believe you've arranged for us to share a room. You have no idea how much this means to me."

Rachel had trouble sleeping that night. As daylight approached, she went downstairs to prepare a cup of tea and saw Claudia asleep on the living-room couch. In the afternoon, while Jenkins sat on the porch, reading contentedly, I gathered up some prickly husks that had fallen from our chestnut tree. It was then that I saw Claudia standing nude at the edge of our pool. She had maintained the slender body of a young girl, though her breasts may have been surgically enhanced. She stood there for a while and may have glanced briefly in my direction. She then executed a perfect dive.

Jenkins called after they'd left to thank us for our hospitality.

"Claudia's returned home. But she's finally agreed, once and for all, to come back and live with me. She only has to settle a few affairs. I think it was your house, your living arrangement, that did the trick. I'm most grateful to you and Rachel."

I said—with sincerity—that I was glad for him. But several weeks later, at dinner, he said that Claudia was having a great deal of difficulty selling her home.

"You'd think it would be an easy matter, but there aren't too many buyers for houseboats. And there's something sticky about the zoning. But she's working hard to get it cleared up. . . ."

And so it went for many years. Claudia was "on the verge" of coming east. There were "plans" for them to tour the great capitals of Europe. And they had "agreed" to buy a house in the country, since Claudia wasn't sure about living in crowded Manhattan. I sympathized with her there. I couldn't imagine anyone living happily in Jenkins's well-located but gray and neglected apartment that was filled with old Ben Jonson folios. I had visited him there once, which was enough.

When I reported these developments, or lack of them, to Rachel, her reaction surprised me, since I'd never known her to be uncharitable.

"I don't care for that woman. And I don't like what she's doing to our friend. She hardly lifts a finger and every need of hers is paid for. She's probably got half a dozen others that she's manipulating in the same way."

Actually, my Czech friend had told me that Claudia had been seen around the Bay Area with a handsomely roguish actor who was known to be an alcoholic.

Still, I felt I had to defend Claudia, and the arrangement.

"Look at it another way. Jenkins gets to pretend he has a family. He's begun to refer to Claudia as his wife, you know. And he doesn't actually have to put up with the complications of living with someone. Down deep he might find that agreeable. He may be a laughingstock to his friends, but he seems perfectly content with the arrangement. Isn't that what counts?"

"I still think she's awful," said Rachel, who had little history of losing arguments. "And don't get any ideas."

I had some work as an assistant director in Mexico, which kept me out of the country for several months. Rachel reached me on the set one day and said that Jenkins had suffered a heart attack. Claudia had flown east to be with him at the hospital. By the time I got home, the doctors had been pleased enough with Jenkins's recovery to release him. Claudia returned to Sausalito.

I visited him at his apartment. He was stretched out on a

worn leather couch, an unlit pipe in his mouth. He seemed pale and emaciated, yet not in the least bit depressed.

"Claudia was absolutely wonderful," he said, a light in his eyes. "She flew here to be with me as soon as she heard of my attack and didn't leave until she saw that I could function on my own. I don't know if I could have pulled through without her. She's found a buyer for her houseboat. Rory is settled at a community college. We agreed that as soon as the sale goes through, she's going to pack up and come to live with me. We'll stay here for a bit, and then we're going to look for a house in New Hampshire."

I mumbled something about it all being good news. Unaccountably, I chose the moment to deny that anything had ever gone on between me and Claudia.

"I know you've long had your suspicions about that time I spent in Sausalito. But whatever you've imagined has been a complete fantasy. I don't know what you've heard or been told. Let me say clearly and emphatically that Claudia and I have never, repeat *never*, had an affair."

I thought for a moment the second "never" might have been a giveaway. But Jenkins seemed not to pick up on it. Calmly, he lit his pipe, which had to be against his doctor's orders.

"Strange that you would bring this up," he said. "The thought never crossed my mind."

Several months passed with no further mention of a houseboat sale and Claudia's planned move to New York. I certainly wasn't going to be the one to introduce the subject.

On Jenkins's eighty-ninth birthday, I treated him to dinner at a pricey French restaurant. He looked ghastly, but at the same time there was something peaceful and resigned about him. He said he'd had a meeting that day with a team of bankers and financial advisers about changes in his will.

"They seemed more concerned than I am about my mortality."

He said this with a chuckle. I wondered if he had accounted for me in the will, though I would have bet heavily against it.

"My sister died recently," he said, nibbling at his food, "and I lost my half-brother last year. That left me without executors. So I've decided to put Claudia in that position."

I said I was surprised he hadn't done so before.

"Made her my *executor?*" he said with surprise. "Now, why on Earth would I do that?"

"She could end up as a very rich lady," I said.

"There are people who have more money than I do. But she should do very nicely."

Several weeks later, Jenkins showed up and was clearly shaken.

"I have the most horrible news. Claudia was packing to make her final trip east—and to move in with me—when she developed a severe headache that turned out to be a brain tumor. She had to have immediate surgery."

I said I couldn't imagine anything more horrible. Sensing that I knew the answer, I asked if he had made arrangements to see her.

"She doesn't want me there," he said. "She's terribly weak and feels she looks awful. She's self-conscious about her hair in particular . . . and there's some short-term memory loss. The feeling is that she'll recover, although it's going to be a long-range process. But when she's back on her feet, everything is in motion for her to join me in Manhattan and for us to live out our years together."

"What can I say? I'll just pray that she has a strong recovery. And if there's anything I can do to help, please let me know."

"Thank you, Derek." He put out a pale and flaccid hand to be shaken. "You've been a good friend."

I reported this new development to Rachel.

"So it's a brain tumor now, is it?" she said, not looking up from her newspaper.

"That's what he said. And why are you putting it that way? You're not suggesting that she's made all this up. Maybe you'd like to see some X-rays."

I thought for a moment. She was silent. She continued to read her newspaper.

"You're being ridiculous," I said. "No one would sink that low. No one on the face of the Earth."

ORANGE SHOES

He noticed her on the first day of summer camp.
And was instantly in love with her.
Sick in love with her.
He was a waiter.
Assigned to wait on her table.
And never said a word to her.
Though she led the girls in teasing him
Each time he brought their food.
"*Oh, Buddy,*" they sang.
"*You must come over, Buddy.*
"*'Cause Gretchen's heart goes pitty-pitty-pat.*
"*There's no one home but the kitty-kitty kat.*
"*Oh, Buddy. Oh Buddy.*
"*You must come over NOW.*"
He thought he'd die of shame.
At night, he watched her dance with others
While he sucked a dry pipe and feigned sophistication.
And remained sick in love with her.
He was sixteen.

A year later
On the first day of summer camp
She pointed at him and said:

"We are going out this summer."
As if to formalize the arrangement
She threw a bottle of black ink at him.
(Ink the color of her hair.)
He brought a tray of food to her table
Then sat on the deck and watched her swim.
Slice through the water in a black bathing suit
The color of her hair.
He was embarrassed by his erection.
She sat on his lap.
In a dripping-wet suit.
While he tried to hide his erection.
He watched her run and dance and shout, her black
   hair flying.
Thinking, *Wild girl.*
Out-of-control girl.
She wrote a catchy song.
Which she played on the piano.
Singing along, her black hair flying.
And he was sick in love with her.

He stole into her cabin one night.
Picked her up in damp pajamas.
Put two fingers in her dry vagina
And carried her off to the woods
Not knowing quite what to do.
Kiss her, smell her damp pajamas.
Keep his fingers in her dry and frightened vagina
Then carry her back to bed.
And leave.
Then stop—and through a window—
Watch her simulate sex with a girlfriend.

The girlfriend on top.
An older girl
A mannish girl who smoked a Russian cigarette.
And seemed world-weary and distracted
Disinterested
Though she thrust her hips out nonetheless.

Another night.
At the edge of the lake.
In a shadowed glade.
He put his fingers in her once again.
And was frightened by the wetness.
Thinking it was over.
Whatever it was.
And that he had caused it to be over.
Before it had begun.

At the season-ending dance, she chose as her date
    another boy.
A butcher boy.
He sat on a bench and watched them.
Then walked outside and looked at the moon.
Her parents arrived at dawn.
To gather up her things and take her home.
They brought along a city friend.
Yet another boyfriend.
Who danced in place and snapped his fingers.
Keeping time to music that only he could hear.
He watched them all drive off.
And sucked his dry pipe.
No longer feigning sophistication.
He left for home soon after.

And fell ill.
Unable to eat or sleep.
Unwilling to eat or sleep.
Unwilling to say why.
Months passed.
He grew pale and thin.
A strong boy, he lost his strength.
An expensive doctor was brought in
And had no answer.
Perhaps the thyroid.
Perhaps not.
And then she phoned one day.
And casually asked if he would meet her in Manhattan.
He agreed to do so.
Matching her casual tone.
And he began to eat and sleep.

He barely recognized her on the street.
She seemed ungainly in a dress.
He had never seen her in a dress.
And she wore orange shoes.
Bright-orange shoes.
Large bright-orange shoes.
Long bright-orange shoes.
Weren't they
In his neighborhood
Referred to as "canal boats"?
All of which he found
Unforgiveable.
They watched a movie.
She said she had her period.
Then added that she would like to be engaged.

He wished her luck.
And said he had his own plan—
To go off to college
In a distant state.
He was aware of his brutality.
His arrogance.
But he was seventeen now.
A boy no more.
And the long bright-orange shoes
The "canal boats"
Had set him free.
He took her to the subway.
Said goodbye.
And never wrote or called.
And became popular at school
By playing and singing a song that she had written.
A catchy song.
With a catchy title.
"Sorry."

THE CHOICE

Courtesy of a botched knee surgery, Gaylord lost the use of eight fingers; two remained intact, almost as a reminder of the good times. His legs were frozen logs. He barely got around on two canes.

"They add dignity," a colleague told him.

But Gaylord knew better. He was a crip. (He knew there was a better term, a more acceptable one, but he was what he was, and it was too late to stand on ceremony.)

Gaylord felt an obligation to stop healthy strangers on the street and warn them not to be too cocky.

"It can happen overnight."

What did he expect them to do, tiptoe cautiously through life?

A risky surgery was proposed.

"The goal is to hold the line," a doctor advised him. "The success rate is sixty percent."

Gaylord didn't dare ask him what happened to the other forty. He knew. And is that what he wanted to shoot for? A chance to stand pat, capping off his life with two canes and a pair of fingers?

Maybe. There were still small pleasures, although, if asked to name them, he had trouble firing off a list. There was the view, of course, from his small apartment close to the river. ("It *leans* on the water," he told his remaining friends.) And he could see the full length of the Hudson. All right, maybe not the *full* length, but a healthy slice of it. And the view changed from morning to night, so that in a sense, he had half a dozen versions of it.

"You have no idea how much that view picks up your spirits," he told those same friends, lording it over them in a way, since most had no view at all.

And it did lift his spirits. Squinting his eyes, he could pretend he was enjoying Lake Como. But how much joy could he wring out of a view? Did that make life worth living? An excellent view of the Hudson?

Hypocritically, though he loathed the politics, he read "Page Six" in the Murdoch *Post* each morning. That was one of his treats. (For his conscience, he balanced it off with the *Times*.) And he had discovered the iPad, so he could get lost in old Warner Bros. movies. Long past worrying about his diet, he ate his favorite breakfast every morning, French toast with blueberries and a thin layer of maple syrup. Miraculously, he remained slender. A widower, Gaylord had a son and a fourteen-year-old granddaughter who lived in Wichita. He enjoyed their occasional visits. In truth, all he could think about during their stay was the fun he could have had with Miriam—when she was a little girl. (And, incidentally, who names a child Miriam these days?)

As he watched traffic go by on the West Side Highway, he considered limping across a small stretch of grass and jumping in front of a homebound Buick. Others had done it. There was no way to get in touch with them, to ask how it had worked out. What was it like on the Other Side? *Was* there an Other Side?

It wasn't his way. Was it anyone's way? Not until the time was ripe. There was no family tradition for him to fall back upon.

Thank God he had his work. An entomologist, he worked in a small research center in lower Manhattan. One thing he could do was hail a cab and give the driver instructions on how to get to Broad Street. For twenty years, he had studied terrestrial vertebrates, publishing a paper now and then, most of them in obscure but highly regarded Finnish journals. Known to a few in the States, Gaylord was a beloved figure in Helsinki. Would his efforts lead to a cure for cancer or some other dread disease? The Finns thought so. Gaylord wasn't so sure. And though he worked assiduously and clung to his research like a lifebuoy, he no longer cared. Forget cancer and Guillain-Barré. His main concern was putting on his pants in the morning. Everything took him ten times longer than it once did. Taking a shower was like building a bridge. Let future generations take care of themselves. Was this selfish? Tell it to his legs and his poor fingers.

One morning, out of the blue, Gaylord received an email from the president of Oulu University saying that he had been awarded the Hanski Award for his outstanding work in the natural sciences. Along with the million-kroner prize money, he would be given a week's stay at the Kämp, one of Helsinki's finest hotels, and, of course, a celebratory banquet attended by all or many of Finland's leading scientists. The previous recipient of the Hanski had donated the cash award for the purchase and preservation of a forest plot in Finland. There was a hint that Gaylord would be expected to do the same—though it was not mandatory. Gaylord was given a week to respond.

His first impulse was to reject the purchase of a forest plot. Maybe, as a token, he'd throw them half an acre. Not that he knew what he would do with the money, which some two-finger tapping on the iPad told him was worth $150,000 in US currency. He could fork it over to his granddaughter, of course, though he continued to have trouble with her name. Wasn't Miriam a name for a grown-up? Of course. That's what had bothered him. And her hyperactivity. Both made her insufferable. He felt better, having figured it out.

Gaylord mulled over the offer and pushed on halfheartedly with his research. One day Brisko, a colleague he rarely spoke to, approached him. He was a small man with a tiny head and a soft and disproportionately wide body. He spoke with a tinny voice. None of this affected his considerable ability as a scientist, but the whole package was unnerving to Gaylord, who kept his distance from the man. When it came to bad bodies, Gaylord lacked saintlike forbearance. Once, irritatingly, Brisko had made a rare appearance at an institute cocktail party with a stunning Asian woman, a head taller than he was. To his dismay, Gaylord was told by a waiter that this was Mrs. Brisko. For the time being and the indefinite future, Gaylord had two canes—and no one to warm his bed. How could he not be envious of his coworker rolling around with a hot Asian.

"I can put some life in those legs of yours," whispered Brisko.

"Please," said Gaylord, "I'm not in the mood for comedy."

"I've never been more serious."

"What have you got, a new doctor?" asked Gaylord, preparing a sample for his microscope. "I've had six."

"No, no, we don't use them."

"We?" asked Gaylord. "Who's we?"

"A small group," said Brisko vaguely.

Since the onset of what he referred to as his "setback," Gaylord felt he was entitled to be rude.

"Get lost," he told his coworker.

Brisko ignored the slight. "See that fellow next to the water cooler," he said.

Gaylord reluctantly looked over at the man, a lab assistant who had just arrived. He wore a blue blazer and gray slacks. "That's Smithers. What about him?"

"*Observez-vous*," said Brisko.

He tapped an old Bunsen burner three times. Smithers's blazer turned gray, his slacks blue. Walking back to his station, Smithers seemed to notice the change. He stopped for a moment, shook his head, as if amused by some cosmic mistake, then continued on his way.

"I'll come right out and ask," said Gaylord. "How the fuck did you do that?"

"That's not the issue," said Brisko. "What's the forecast? For the next two days?"

Ritualistically, Gaylord checked the weather each morning on his computer.

"Sunshine, from dawn till sundown."

"Wrong," said Brisko with uncharacteristic sharpness, causing several interns to whip their heads around. Then he went back to a whisper.

"Prepare for record-breaking thunderstorms, on both days, from noon to midnight. I'll speak to you on Thursday. And by the way, Changchang sends her regards."

"Your wife?" asked Gaylord.

"Who else would it be? You think I fool around?"

The sun was blinding the next morning. As he left his apartment, Gaylord threw up a hand to block it out and felt lucky to reach the air-conditioned safety of a Yellow cab. Later, when he left the lab to get a sandwich, the rain came down with such force it not only soaked his tuna on rye but threatened to drown him. The following day began promisingly, with clear skies. But as if scheduled, torrential rains came down precisely at noon, destroying the more cautious Gaylord's fine (and expensive) British umbrella.

On the third day, Brisko greeted Gaylord at his workstation.

"Care to see some card tricks?"

"Never mind," said Gaylord. "I get it, I get it."

But as he said this, Brisko pulled a straight flush out of a nostril.

"Oh, Jesus," said Gaylord, who was touchy in this area. "No nose stuff, all right? Now, how's it work?"

"I can have you springy in a couple of days."

Gaylord hated himself for developing confidence in the man. "What about the fingers?"

"Four, maybe five tops. Fingers are negotiable."

"And tennis?"

"Doubles," said Brisko emphatically.

"I'll take it," said Gaylord, who could almost hear the thwack of a ball against his racket, a favorite sound.

"There's a condition," said Brisko, lowering his head.

Had he suddenly become shy?

"Isn't there always? Lay it on me."

"There's to be no prize."

"No Finns?" said Gaylord. "No Helsinki?"

"You can visit, of course. Take in the clubs, the forests. But no award."

"So I'll be springy and unrecognized."

"You've summed it up beautifully. The best part is you have twenty-four hours to mull it over."

"Why is that the best part?" asked Gaylord thoughtfully.

Brisko looked hurt. "We thought it was rather generous."

"Right back at you," said Gaylord, a phrase he'd heard in the streets, and one he never dreamed of using. "Tomorrow morning. And incidentally, Brisko, what do you get out of this?"

"The pleasure of watching you squirm."

"You're not a good person," said Gaylord.

"And you're no angel."

Gaylord didn't waste a minute. After cleaning up his lab table, he left the building and hit the ground mulling. To get some spring in his lifeless legs! And say goodbye to the nickname he'd given himself: "Dead Legs." To get back on the tennis court, even though he hated losing and slept restlessly the night before a meaningless match. He'd had his eye on a comely young intern. Long blond hair, a nightclub voice. She came to work in short black skirts, then changed into a lab coat. And oh, those legs. He'd exchanged (choked out) a few words with her, then backed away for fear she'd spot the canes. With the legs back under him and the return of most, but not all, of his fingers, the sky was the limit. Drinks, dinner. Maybe he'd have his own Changchang. And travel. He'd be able to *say* the word "wheelchair," since he'd have no use for one. Shanghai was high on his list, although, in truth, he'd read a long piece on shopping in the *New Yorker* on Shanghai and felt he had already been there.

The new—or the restored—Gaylord would be able to walk the three blocks to his local supermarket. Admittedly, they were only trustworthy on staples—bread, butter, and eggs. But the great Zabar's itself was within reach. No need to get carried away, but what was to stop him from biking along the path that lay mockingly alongside the Hudson? More than once, he'd made it to the Holocaust Memorial and back without losing his breath.

What a deal. And it had fallen right into his lap. By the time he'd gotten out of the cab, he'd made up his mind. He'd call the lab and tell the weird little Brisko to start the ball rolling. He was on board. After that, he'd send an email to the Finns expressing his regrets.

He was confident he'd made the right decision. Only a fool would trade his legs for a prize. Yet he had some doubts. . . .

For years Gaylord had worked in anonymity. When a colleague was singled out for a prize, he felt little envy and was among the first to offer his congratulations. Let his own experiments go well. That was his reward. He'd learned of a dying colleague who yearned for laurels. Gaylord wondered: What does he need them for? So he can drop dead grinning?

Still, Gaylord was essentially a normal person. What would be so terrible about a little applause? With an absence of recognition, he would end his life as if he'd never existed. A speck (if he was lucky) in the Great Void. With the Hanski under his belt, he'd still be a speck, but one with a little glitter to it.

The Hanski was not the Nobel. Gaylord didn't need to be told that. Still, he assumed there would be a Great Hall. How could there not be? There were all those Finnish scientists, more per capita than any country. (They'd nosed out Germany.) He envisioned a procession of distinguished Finns, Gaylord being wheeled along by a uniformed attendant. There would be an ovation, not thunderous—the Finns were known to be stolid—but impressive nonetheless. Would Einstein himself be impervious to such a reception?

Gaylord began to compose an acceptance speech. It would be anchored in a salute to humanity—how could it not?—and then would branch off to the wonders of science and the universe, with a special tip of the cap to the Finns, who had so often shown the way. Had they really? For the time being, this was of no importance.

As if sensing that he was squirming around indecisively, the Finns sent a follow-up email assuring him that the Helsinki press would be there in full force. Denmark would be on board as well. How could the *New York Times* itself ignore such an event? Gaylord lived in a world of test tubes and tissue samples. He knew little of YouTube. Yet if they had any sense, they would pay attention.

There would be limousines at his beck and call. Attached to the follow-up email was a photograph of his "attendant," a lissome blonde with an advanced degree in—what else—Gaylord's beloved entomology. The Finns weren't fools.

Their offer was more than tempting. And Gaylord could still get around with the canes. In truth, he needed only one. But he'd seen a photograph of Norman Mailer, a literary hero, limping along with two, so he ordered an extra.

Biking had become tiresome. Did he need another visit to the Holocaust Museum? He'd visited five. When you'd seen Yad Vashem, you'd seen them all.

Tennis, in truth, took too great a toll on his nervous system. Worrying all the time. What if he lost? And did he really need to eat fried grasshoppers in Shanghai?

His fingers? He could hunt and peck on the computer. If he suddenly felt an urge to do a memoir, he could, with presumption, dictate, like Churchill.

He'd stayed away from the theatre. The crowds. An aisle seat cost a fortune. And what was there to see? *Mary Poppins*?

Despite his disability, he still had his books, his papers, his bottle of wine, seven o'clock on the dot, along with crackers and a strong cheese. He'd discovered a local takeout place that delivered linguini with fresh—repeat, fresh—clams.

And let's not forget his guilty pleasure—*Law & Order: Special Victims Unit.*

He thought again of the Great Hall, the banquet, the ovation from the usually stolid Finns, the light-haired (and worshipful) attendant. To turn his back on the first recognition he'd ever gotten. A chance to step out of the darkness. To step out of his hole. To stop feigning delight when a colleague won an award. To take a turn in the spotlight before the lights went out for good. To have an answer for the laboratory wise-ass who teased him in the men's room.

"Still under the radar, Gaylord?"

To trade all this away?

Once again, he called Brisko and left a succinct message on his voicemail. One no doubt influenced by the dialogue in old Warner Bros. movies:

"Get yourself another boy."

He signed off: "The Gimp."

An email to Helsinki went out next.

"Count me in."

Gaylord glanced at the clock. It wasn't quite seven. Still he permitted himself to open a bottle of wine, to pour a glass and settle back in his favorite armchair, one with a clean view of his beloved Hudson. His two canes leaned against a bookcase. And for the first time since the surgery, he could have sworn he felt a lifelike tingle in his legs.

NIGHTGOWN

Stranded in Manhattan on a holiday weekend, Nat Solomon, a visiting academic from Detroit, decided to treat himself to an off-Broadway play. The production had received tepid reviews, but the theme intrigued him. The plot? A Catholic priest had begun to doubt his faith. Rather than speak to his bishop—he'd been there before—he decided to reach beyond the Church and to consult a psychiatrist.

Solomon himself had lost three of them; that is to say, a trio of psychiatrists had died on his watch. They were old men; he had sought them out for their wisdom. Never had it occurred to Solomon that one by one they would expire, which they did—just as he was getting somewhere. He took another try—this time with a Jungian. When she learned of the three dead shrinks, she turned color and refused to take him on as a patient.

At the moment, Solomon had no one. When it came to his mental health, he was flying solo, barely holding his life together—a distant wife, a rudderless daughter, shrinking income, and crumbling knees. It was quite a package.

Solomon lucked out and got an aisle seat in the tiny theater—the better to stretch out his left knee, the one that was in the first position on pain. Both performers in the two-character play were accomplished, but Solomon could not take his eyes off the actor who played the psychiatrist. Never before had he seen such compassion in the face of a therapist. Each time the priest cried out in anguish, the therapist cried out with him, though silently, if such a thing were possible. The few times he spoke, his words trembled with humility and quiet strength, a difficult combination to pull off. Solomon waited for him to stroke his chin, an unbearable cliché. Stroke it he did, although the stroke was closer to the ear than the chin, which made a world of difference. When he drummed his fingers on a desk, Solomon did some drumming of his own—on the armrest. The priest had been waffling. The drumming was a gentle nudge. Get to the heart of what's eating you.

There was a slight trace of Cockney in the psychiatrist's voice, which was appealing. There was a puckish grin in the mix. All of it was irresistible.

In the last scene of the brief play, the priest, beaming with fresh perspective, wrote out a check and blessed his fellow actor. Solomon would have done the same. Both performers received a standing ovation.

Where do you find such a man, Solomon wondered as he left the theater. With all respect to the three psychiatrists he'd buried and a few he'd met at parties, not one had the quality of the man he'd seen on the stage. He was convinced that such an individual could finally set him on the path to mental health.

There were few restaurants in the darkened neighborhood. Solomon decided to have a bite in a tavern that virtually leaned against the theater. Flanagan's, it was called. How bad could it be? No sooner had he wolfed down a cheeseburger than the actor he so admired entered the restaurant, took a seat near the kitchen, and whipped out a copy of *Variety*. Solomon took a swallow of his beer and approached the gifted thespian.

"Forgive me for intruding," said Solomon, "but I thought your performance was brilliant."

The actor looked up with a smile.

"That's very kind," he said, then returned to his show-biz newspaper.

"I hope you don't find this indelicate," said Solomon, who was slightly offended that he'd been so quickly ignored, "but may I ask you how much you earn—performing in a play like this? The question is in a good cause. I don't mean to offend."

The actor looked up again. "We don't get rich, that's for sure. Actually we get a percentage of the gate. I made about seventy bucks tonight."

"What if I gave you a thousand?" said Solomon, getting in the question before the actor returned to *Variety.*

"For what?"

"For doing essentially what you do onstage. I'm not a rich man. I'm a professor of anthropology, but it would be well worth it to me. What's more important than our mental health?"

"I agree with you on that."

The actor took a close look at Solomon.

"This isn't a gay thing, is it?"

"No. Of course not."

And then he felt compelled to add, with a chuckle, "Certainly not to my knowledge."

The actor set aside his newspaper.

"I'm sure you're aware that I didn't write the play. I do vamp a bit here and there, to keep the performance fresh, to keep up my interest, frankly. But the dialogue was written by the playwright Ruth Bender-Farkas, and I rarely stray from it."

"Bender-Farkas would be nothing without you," said Solomon.

The actor accepted the compliment without protest.

"How exactly would this work?"

"On a night that you're not performing, I'd come up to your place—my hotel room wouldn't be a good idea. I'd ask you to simply sit at your desk—much as you do in the play—and listen."

"I don't have a desk."

"A coffee table will do."

"How long would this take?" asked the actor.

"An hour."

He corrected himself. "Fifty minutes. The usual."

"The whole thing's ridiculous," said the actor in a sudden change of mood.

Once again, he returned to *Variety*.

Solomon forgave him. After all, the man was an artist, subject to sudden flashes of temperament.

He reached into his pocket, counted out $500, and slapped it on the table.

"What about this?" he said.

It was all of his travel money—but there was an ATM in the hotel and at least another $500 in his account.

The actor stared at the money. Then he picked it up, not quite counting it, but giving it a quick riffle. He put it in his pocket.

"We don't have a performance on Sundays. Does that work for you?"

"Perfectly."

"Shall I prepare some lunch?"

"No, no, that would spoil it."

The actor lived in a fifth-story walk-up—a single room with a small kitchen and a surprisingly formidable collection of books. One, Solomon couldn't help noting, was a biography of Sammy Davis Jr. But *The Best of Spinoza* was on an adjoining shelf. Interesting man, thought Solomon. Not just an actor. Of course, he'd surmised as much. The actor had, unnecessarily Solomon felt, prepared a snack—crackers covered with peanut butter. Perhaps getting into character, he showed Solomon to the coffee table with a thin and serious smile, then sat opposite him, crossing his legs demurely. Solomon thought: This is exactly the way to begin.

Not wanting to be rude, Solomon chomped down one of the peanut-butter snacks. A drink would have been useful, to wash it past his dry throat, but why waste time and ask? Thinking it only fair, he began by telling the actor of the three psychiatrists who had died while Solomon was in mid-treatment. One had expired quietly in his chair, just as Solomon was about to kick off a session. Surprisingly composed, Solomon had called 911. After the police had questioned him, he had respectfully faded away and written a letter to the man's widow. Only in the weeks that followed did Solomon grieve.

Three psychiatrists. Each one dead and gone. There was a slight flicker of concern on the actor's face, and why wouldn't there be. But then that, too, faded away.

"It would be ego to think I had anything to do with the deaths, don't you feel?"

The actor shrugged and spread out his hands, palms up, as if to say, *How can we tell? If only we had the answer to such questions.*

A perfect response, thought Solomon.

He continued: "The last doctor who bit the dust felt it was important to deal with my feelings about money."

Bit the dust. Solomon was aware he'd used an attention-getting phrase, a little jokey, perhaps to defuse the pain he'd felt when he'd lost Mel Glickman, an important figure in his life.

"And then of course the prostate caught up with him.

Brilliant man. Brave too. Continued his practice to the end, although it was hell to see him squirming around in the chair. I could barely concentrate."

Was it possible that the actor winced and did a little reactive squirm in his own chair? Such empathy, Solomon felt. Incredible.

He continued along. "So we never did get around to covering money, although something strange just happened, just now, right here in your apartment."

The actor's eyes widened a bit, with what seemed to be authentic curiosity.

"For the first time, I flashed on my mother's first words to me about money. I was a boy of five."

And now the actor leaned forward, chin in hand, an elbow on his knee.

"'Money means nothing to me,' she said. 'It's crap.'

"The implication was that there are more important things in life—family, for example, although ours wasn't so terrific. But I ask you—is that why I can hardly wait to dispose of money on those rare occasions when I have some? So I can wash my hands, metaphorically, and get rid of the crap?"

The actor seemed doubtful. He did a half shrug this time, then reversed himself by looking thoughtfully off in the distance, not stroking his chin but holding it. Then he nodded, almost imperceptibly, as if to say, *You may be on to something.*

"Great," said Solomon. "That's exactly how I feel. I'm so relieved to finally clear up my confusion about money."

He shook his head in wonder. "After three psychiatrists, and all these long years, you just come along and bam, you nail it."

The actor flashed an authentically charming smile. Solomon noticed for the first time how handsome he was. Why wasn't he a star? Possibly he was a late bloomer. Solomon had a friend at the Morris Agency in Los Angeles. But this was not the time to get involved in the man's career.

"Then there's the death thing," Solomon continued, "something else we didn't cover. I've never been able to quite get my arm around mortality. You live and you die and that's it. Or, fat chance, there's something beyond, an afterlife."

The actor expelled a little air from his nose, producing a snuffling sound. Solomon felt he could read the man's mind.

The great thinkers of history have been grappling with that question for centuries. Don't beat yourself up. You're not alone.

"You're right on that," said Solomon, although, in truth, the actor hadn't actually said anything. "There's religion, of course, and God bless the folks who take comfort from it. I actually keep a copy of *Ten Great Religions* on my night table . . . but with each one of the faiths, there's always that leap you have to make, or you'll never get off the dime. And I can't take that leap. To make it worse, I don't even have a comforting philosophy. At my age, sixty-two, you'd think I'd have one. Maggy, that's my wife, says, 'Don't worry, Nat. You'll get one when you need it.' I just love her for that."

Solomon almost added: "Don't you?"

The actor responded with an ingratiating smile and a little shake of his head. The message he seemed to be sending?

You're a lucky man to have a woman like that in your life.

"I agree," said Solomon. "And I am so thrilled that you and I are doing this. It's worked out exactly the way I had planned."

The actor smiled again and nodded humbly, as if satisfied that he'd done a good job.

Solomon glanced up at the kitchen clock and was surprised, alarmed actually, to see how much time had gone by. He felt he'd barely cleared his throat. And yet he'd eaten up a good slice of the session. He could ask for another hour, of course, maybe a half, assuming the actor didn't have to attend a rehearsal or something. But this would seriously strain his budget. So he decided to cram as much nagging conflict as possible into what was left of the session.

As if he'd read Solomon's thoughts, the actor too glanced at the clock. He did a little roll of one hand as if to say, might as well get on with it.

In a great rush, Solomon tackled his loss of tenure, his daughter's arrest for shoplifting, a bitter argument with his oldest friend, and his EKG, the one that had frightened two nurses.

The actor tried to keep up the pace with nods of under-standing, flat-out chin strokes, encouraging grins, and an occasional frown, albeit a sympathetic one. But finally he held up his hand. He'd had enough. When he spoke, for the first time, his voice was soft and modulated, but it might as well have been a clap of thunder.

"I have to stop you here. We're almost out of time. How can I help you? What do you want from me?"

"Exactly what you've been doing. And I was hoping we'd get back to my mother. I believe it's germane."

He paused a moment to make sure the actor was familiar with the word.

The actor grinned, nodded.

Somewhat reassured, Solomon pressed on.

"She was awfully smart, but she didn't know what to do with herself. Once a year, she'd make a big deal over paint-ing our tiny apartment in the Bronx. She was ten times more intelligent than my father, who worked in the garment center, and she clearly should have been the one who was out in the field while he stayed home. But that would have been emasculating. Or so went the culture. So she stayed in the apartment and brooded. Each morning, after she had a cup of coffee, she would hail a cab on the Grand Concourse in the Bronx and tell the driver to just drive, it didn't matter where. And she would talk for about an hour, essentially what we're doing. Then she'd come home feeling better, even looking refreshed. All this, first thing in the morning, and she hadn't even gotten out of her nightgown. . . ."

"Her nightgown . . ." the actor repeated thoughtfully.

"That's what I said. Her nightgown. What point are you making?"

The actor did a modest shrug. It was just a thought.

Solomon reflected for a moment.

"Oh, *I* see what you're getting at. Why didn't she get dressed? She did more than *talk* in that cab. Is that what you're saying? That really is a low blow. Completely beneath you, actually."

Unsettled, Solomon took a moment to pull himself together.

"I'll concede she was a little flirtatious—there was one time in Miami when I was twelve years old and I walked in on her and the hotel manager. Who knows what they were up to. Come to think of it, there was something about a comedian in Monticello. It was probably nothing. The same thing with the insurance man.

"But first thing in the morning? In her nightgown? In the backseat? My *mother*? *Mom*? Who spit blood when she had me? Made believe she was chewing food when *I* chewed as if to make sure I didn't choke? Stayed up all night, putting hot compresses on my foot when there was a suspicion that a wound might be gangrenous? All the while mumbling to herself, 'This is my lot. What did I expect? I'm a mother.'

She gave up theatre tickets to a Broadway show that night. Handed them to the doorman. A hit musical. And what do *you* do, gonif? Throw her under a bridge, nightgown at her neck, legs splayed, rolling around in the grass with a strange cabdriver. While my poor father goes blind sewing shoulder pads on Seventh Avenue."

Near tears from that last image, Solomon got to his feet. Only the knee kept him from leaping over the coffee table to get his hands on the man.

"I have to give you credit. You are some sonofabitch. Why I ever trusted you I'll never know. You're not getting the other five hundred."

"You go too far, sir," said the actor, suddenly out of character, taking on a role he'd played in a Restoration comedy.

"Not another dime," said Solomon, starting for the door.

He stopped and called back.

"You're a lousy actor too. I can see why you're working in toilets.

"And I guarantee you this," said Solomon, with a theatrical flourish of his own. "You will *never* make it to Broadway."

THE STRAINER

I'd always wondered what it would be like to give a party in the apartment—we'd only lived there for a year—and then all of a sudden I found out, except that it wasn't the guest list I'd had in mind. There were four tall, polite cops drinking coffee I'd gotten from the Palestinians in the all-night gourmet deli on Seventh Avenue. And a whole flock of emergency workers who were crowded around Jenny, trying to find out how it happened.

"Were you on the john?" one of them asked.

"Straining . . . ?" another put in helpfully.

Apparently, a lot of people in Manhattan have heart attacks when they're straining on the john. It wouldn't surprise me if they actually called them "strainers." After a little coaxing, Jenny admitted that she was one of them, and once she got that out of the way she was off to the races. They got stuff out of her you'd have to torture someone like me to admit. Was she a smoker? Uh-huh. Drinker? You bet. Any family history of coronary disease? Absolutely—a whole ton of it, mostly on the male side, dating way back to the grandfather who was a wrestler in Skokie, Illinois.

She didn't have to tell them about the thirty pounds she'd put on—they did have eyes. What surprised me is that she didn't fill them in on the dope we smoked that was supposed to bring you to a New Level where the thirty, actually forty, pounds didn't matter and it was all right if it took you till Shavuot to get your dick in gear. And it worked too. I don't know what I'm complaining about. But we had an agreement to only use it on Saturday night, and I know for a fact that Jenny was sneaking puffs of it all week long during *Seinfeld* reruns. How she got on the subway to Bensonhurst the next morning to counsel troubled Pakistanis is beyond me.

The dope was one thing, but when you put it together with the six-packs and the fried this and fried that, not to mention the Nat Sherman Cigaratellos, it was no surprise she was hooked up to twenty different kinds of monitors and being asked if she was a strainer. The woman who held the IV equipment said she loved the apartment. Jenny thanked her and said it would look better when we painted it.

"We're thinking of French yellow."

The IV woman made a face—she wasn't so sure about French yellow—but it was great that she loved the apartment. We had the high ceilings and the whole loft effect, but I was a little insecure about the view, since all you could really see was a bunch of people in the next building bent over tables doing graphic design. Actually, you could make out a little bit of the Chrysler Building, but you'd have to stand way over in the corner near the bookshelves and get up on your toes. And you have to remember we came from fourteen rooms and a huge spread right down the road from the ocean. All right, it was Nova Scotia, but still, we had all that space and the cragginess and we were a little spoiled. Anyway, I loved the new building, the doormen, the area. It didn't even bother me that there were all those blind people running around and every third store sold office chairs and that Zagat called our neighborhood "The Dead Zone." As far as I was concerned, that added character. I just didn't want to live there alone.

The woman who loved the apartment said they had to take Jenny over to Lenox Hill—just to be on the safe side. Jenny asked me to pack some things for her and to make sure I included fresh panties. Why she had to throw in the "fresh" part is beyond me. Actually, it related to a joke of ours. "I got you some fresh coffee." Or "I brought you a fresh *Daily News.*" It's the kind of routine you have to be married to someone for a couple of decades to appreciate. It's not like you pick somebody up at a club, spend the night with them, and start doing that kind of material the next morning. But the ER people didn't know any of this and they probably thought that Jenny had two sets of panties—fresh and not-so-fresh.

I asked the blood-pressure guy if he could step aside so I could get to Jenny's dresser. And then I remembered there had been a mix-up and our laundry had been delivered to the yenta in 6B who had questioned my decency. He'd been lying in wait for me next to the salad bar at D'Agostino's.

"Have you no decency?" he said.

And he said it with a lisp too—I'm sorry, I can't help that— so that it came out *de-thency.* Evidently, Gary, the Portuguese water dog, had barked at two o'clock in the morning (2:10, the yenta wrote it down) and cost the guy a whole night's sleep. I didn't hear any of this, since I always insert Mack's Earplugs to counteract Jenny's snoring. But I took his word for it and apologized, although frankly I didn't appreciate my decency being called into question. What was I supposed to do, start listing my charitable contributions? You can't win that one, so I said I'd see what I could do, which was very little, since Gary had just come in from Nova Scotia and he probably missed the salt air. He hadn't settled in to the city yet. The neighbor swanned off—my new word—and the next day the building manager handed me a petition saying I was spoiling the quality of life of the tenant in 6B. He had gotten four of his yenta friends to sign it, saying I was spoiling *their* quality of life as well. Well, I really lost it, right out there in the lobby.

"What about *my* quality of life? Have you seen the trash that guy drags in here every night? This was supposed to be a *family* building. It was in the brochure."

And then the second I said that, I felt awful. For one thing, even though we didn't have long discussions about it, Jenny and I knew the building was a little gay. Sixty percent, easy. And there was a contingent who you didn't know what they were. It wasn't an issue. As to my neighbor, it's true he had a new partner every twenty minutes, but they were basically clean-cut, decent-looking individuals. There was one ratty-looking guy with a moth-eaten beard, but even he could have been some kind of academic. Or maybe it was a cousin. So I apologized to the building manager, who said he was only doing his job. I didn't even get into a whole Eichmann thing. He went off muttering, "There's one in every building," and I didn't know if he was talking about *me* or the neighbor. He was terrific at being neutral, which is probably why they hired him and gave him the free apartment.

I was so upset by the experience that I made an appointment with the rabbi. He's not really a rabbi, he's a shrink who's Orthodox and wears a yarmulke, which threw me off in the consultation. Actually, it was Jenny who found him, but she didn't prepare me for the yarmulke. He charges $385 an hour, and where he got that figure I'll never know. I'd say it was in the Diamond District if it wasn't so blatantly anti-Semitic. On the other hand, I was used to Nova Scotia prices, where every-thing costs forty cents. And he *is* good. Very bottom-line. He doesn't want to hear about the uncle who grabbed your dick at a Mets game—that's history, let's get on with it. Actually, that's

Jenny's style too, with the troubled Pakistanis, and if she had just sat with me for a few minutes I could have saved the three eighty-five. But apparently there's some rule that says you can't treat your husband. So with regard to my neighbor, what the rabbi basically told me for the three-eight-five was to forget it. And I more or less did. The next time I met the guy in the elevator I gave him a haughty look and thought that was the end of it. Except that now I had to knock on his door and say he had Jenny's panties. Assuming the cocksucker wasn't wearing them.

In the meanwhile, I packed a few twisty little panties that probably hadn't fit Jenny since she was a cheerleader at Ball State. How she managed to combine cheerleading with a doctorate in Far East studies is a mystery to me. I threw in a toothbrush, a couple of face creams, and an Irish novel that I warned Jenny was all texture but that she insisted on buying anyway. I was looking under the bed for a flannel nightie when it occurred to me that this whole episode was real—it wasn't a rehearsal for *Hedda Gabler*—and there was nothing in the drawer to calm me down. We had a new doctor who practically threw pills at you when you walked in the door, but he refused to give me anything for anxiety. He'd seen me on a panel show, the one time I was really on my game. I was wailing—nobody could get a word in.

"I can't give you anything," he said. "You're a national treasure."

So as a result of him thinking I was a national treasure, everyone in the city was running around with some kind of happy pill except me.

What I was worried about primarily is that I'd faint and they'd have to make room for me on the stretcher. I have a little history in this area. I'd almost keeled over recently during a backer's audition for a movie about chemo high-jumpers. It was just raw footage, but it was pretty powerful stuff with the ironic soundtrack from Aerosmith, and I barely made it through the credits.

Somebody on the ER team said it was time to get moving and I didn't even have time to think about fainting. The next thing I knew, all fourteen of us were parading past the doorman from Chechnya and they were sliding Jenny into the ambulance and I was thinking, Hey wait a minute, where are you going, where are you taking her? Don't you understand, don't you get it . . . that's my girl.

We were out in Quogue. Peaceful. Jenny was in a chair. I can't bring myself to say "wheelchair." I fed her, changed her, washed her skinny legs. I read to her. "Page Six," *The Economist*. We took walks along the ocean, Gary trotting behind us. Then back to the fireside. It wasn't a bad life—nothing to write home about—but hey, as I say, she's my girl.

THE SAVIOR

He was a stout and indolent-looking man who appeared to be in his mid-fifties, a bit older than Lowell. He could usually be found on the porch of the small resort hotel or beside the lake, sitting in a chair and dozing. Not to be unkind about it, but Lowell felt he looked like a giant bullfrog, lazing in the sun. Yet for a reason he couldn't fathom, Lowell was drawn to the man.

It took some time for Lowell to realize, however implausibly, that this was the person who had torn the heart out of his first marriage, destroyed his family, and virtually ruined his life.

Lowell's second wife, June, had found Pinewood Lakes on the web, listed under "weekend getaways." The tiny resort community was an hour and ten minutes' drive from Manhattan. Yet the contrast with the city was dramatic. The air was fresh and invigorating. As a boy, Lowell had been sent to summer camps in Maine and New Hampshire. He'd forgotten how much he missed the lake country—and the crisp mountain air.

Though the room they were shown to in the small hotel was cramped, the manager tried to put a good face on it.

"It was a favorite," he said, "of the late, great Lou Gehrig, one of your baseball icons."

For all of the freshness of their surroundings, they soon

discovered that there wasn't much for them to do in the way of activities. The lake was a bit too chilly for swimming. The bike path that ran along the highway was narrow and dangerously close to traffic. The one restaurant in the nearby town featured German-style cooking that was decent but nothing to write home about. Lowell suggested they take a hike through the woods. June gamely went along with him, but she was unenthusiastic about it. To get to her job as a schoolteacher in Brooklyn, she had to take long walks back and forth to the subway each day. That, and standing on her feet all day long, was exercise enough for her. And June was much more self-contained than Lowell. She was content to cozy down beside the lake with her mystery novels—and to go to bed early.

By the end of the second day of their four-day vacation, Lowell, an entertainment lawyer, was restless. At nine o'clock at night, he found himself sitting in the hotel lobby with one disinterested eye on the tiny television set. A heavyset and heavy-lidded guest was sitting on an adjacent sofa. As it turned out, he wasn't dozing at all. Lowell could not recall who it was that was the first to speak. But suddenly they were chatting away. The man's name was Peter Neely. He had grown up in the same Bronx neighborhood as Lowell, though Neely had attended Catholic schools and Lowell was a public school graduate. They had both come from poor, if not impoverished, families, although they agreed it made them feel wealthy to live within walking distance of two Major League ballparks, Yankee Stadium and the Polo Grounds. Neely wasn't in the least bit indolent. His memory was as clear and sharp as the mountain air. He was able to recite the entire lineup of the New York Yankees of the period—and that of the New York Giants before they were moved to San Francisco. A printer by trade, Neely lived in Garden City, Long Island. He and his wife had been guests of the little hotel for at least a decade. They came up in summer and winter. On this occasion, Mrs. Neely had chosen to visit her sister in Lauderdale. Neely had come up alone.

Lowell warmed to the man even more when it turned out that Neely had a strong interest in serious theatre and in contemporary British fiction as well. Both men were huge fans of Anthony Powell. Neely had read the early works of the great novelist—the ones before the famed "Dance" series. Lowell hadn't—and scribbled down their titles so that he could order them when he got back to the city.

After they had been chatting for an hour or so, Neely said that he often stayed in Manhattan for dinner after work.

"I wonder if you'd care to join me one night," he asked.

Lowell said he'd be delighted.

"Do you know of a restaurant in the Village called Gene's?"

"It's one of my favorites."

"Suppose I call you one day," said Neely, "and we meet there for dinner?"

"It's a deal," said Lowell.

Lowell was pleased with his new "find." He had recently lost several close friends. His remaining ones—acquaintances, really—were writers, agents, lawyers, all of them connected to the entertainment field. He had often wondered what it would be like to know a normal person, a "real American," so to speak—though he was aware of a whiff of patronization in this feeling. Perhaps more than a whiff. For the remainder of the trip, Lowell waved to Neely whenever he saw him but did not stop to speak to him—as if afraid to jeopardize their budding friendship. When Neely called, a week after their encounter, Lowell agreed to meet him at Gene's restaurant.

The conversation at dinner was stiff at first, but each man loosened up quickly after a few cocktails. Lowell told his new friend that he and June had lived in Manhasset for many years and only recently moved back to Manhattan.

"I love every precious second of it."

Neely spoke of his college years at Loyola and his late—and childless—marriage to Eunice. It was only when he brought up his early years as a limousine driver and his work as manager of a small bookshop in Chelsea that Lowell began to suspect that he had met his dinner partner many years before. He became convinced of it when Neely mentioned that he had once translated the work of an obscure German essayist named Hans Wollschläger. There was no question about it. No two individuals could have had the same background. The man who sat opposite Lowell had once wrecked his life. For years, he had thought of him as a mortal enemy.

"Was your name ever McNeely?" asked Lowell.

"Yes. I decided to tighten it up a bit."

"And we knew each other, didn't we? Before we met at Pinewood."

"It's entirely possible," said Neely neutrally, polishing off a giant shrimp with a single bite.

Lowell felt a coldness at the back of his neck and across his shoulders. Was it possible that Neely knew in advance of Lowell's visit to Pinewood—and had shown up at the resort in order to taunt him? This was highly unlikely. Lowell and his wife had decided to get away for a weekend on the spur of the moment. No one else could have known about their trip. Did

Neely know of their past connection now? If so, when did he first become aware of it?

What to do? One option was to rise above the battle, so to speak, and simply get up and leave, washing his hands of the whole business. After all, hadn't it all happened long before, in what seemed like another life? For the time being, Lowell decided to go ahead with his dinner. He ordered a porterhouse steak.

"I'll try the striped sea bass," said Neely.

Before the main courses were served, the waiter placed a sharp steak knife beside Lowell's dinner plate. There was a time when he would have plunged it into Neely's chest without hesitation. Lowell had left his office one night with a lead pipe in his pocket, determined to seek out Neely and crush his skull. Lowell had told his story to a partner in the firm who had stopped him at the door.

"It's not worth it," said the old barrister.

But it had seemed worth it at the time.

Lowell had only the dimmest recollection of the young Neely's appearance. He vaguely recalled a man who was tall, sharp-featured, and wore a cap.

Years back, to celebrate their anniversary, Lowell and his first wife, Sylvia, had hired a limousine to take them from Oyster Bay to a dance party in the West Village. A group of friends awaited them. On the way to Manhattan, they began chatting with the driver, who turned out to have a literary bent. With his eyes on the road, he quoted Rilke and the work of a lesser-known writer named Wollschläger. Though Lowell didn't much care for Champagne, he and Sylvia drank quite a bit of it on the way to Manhattan. Since they were both charmed by the driver, it made perfectly good sense at the time to invite him along to the party. Once there, Lowell left his wife in the hands of the limo driver and slipped away in pursuit of women. His marriage was shaky. He and Sylvia did not get along in bed. As a result, he was always on the lookout for a possible affair. Nothing of the kind came about that night. They took a train back to Oyster Bay, paid the babysitter, then slipped into a loveless bed. A week later, Lowell received a gracious note from the limo driver—McNeely—thanking the couple for a lovely evening. A week after that, Lowell was taken aside at a cocktail party by an alleged friend of Sylvia's.

"Aren't you shocked?" said the friend, eyes sparkling. "How can she do this?"

"Do what?" asked Lowell.

"Have an affair . . . with a limo driver?"

Lowell felt as if he'd been shot through the chest. Too upset to wait until they got home, he confronted Sylvia at the cocktail party. Was it true?

"Yes," she said, in the defiant manner of heroines in Victorian novels.

"You'll have to break it off immediately."

"That's impossible," she said.

Sick at heart, and barely able to stay on the road, Lowell drove his wife home in silence. For the next several days, they said nothing more of the affair. Lowell moved from the master bedroom to the attic. Late at night, he would see a yellow light on the second line of the attic phone and he knew his wife was talking to the limo man. (Lowell stubbornly refused to use his name.) He covered the phone light with a pillow, but he knew it was on and that they were talking, sometimes for hours. Only when he checked and saw that the light had gone off was he able to get to sleep.

His wife refused to discuss the affair. Maddeningly, she traveled in to the city on "shopping" trips. Though Lowell couldn't bring himself to contact McNeely on the phone, he plotted ways to kill him. Not hurt him. Kill him. Lowell's wife said that the limo man was aware of Lowell and his intentions and had moved in with a friend who served as a bodyguard. Lowell planned to kill them both. He told his wife that he was not going to move out or file for divorce until the girls were on their feet. They were ten and eleven.

"But once I decide to leave, there is no force on Earth that will keep me here."

In truth, he was afraid to be alone, afraid to be abandoned.

He amazed himself by continuing to be effective at his work, negotiating contracts for comedians. Each night, he drove back to Oyster Bay on the Long Island Expressway and waited for Sylvia to return from one of her "shopping" trips to Manhattan. He began a halfhearted affair of his own, taking advantage of a solemn pottery instructor, though he knew they had no future. He felt a certain contempt for himself. To hide his face, he grew a beard. Then one day he shaved it off and saw a divorce lawyer.

"Did she withhold sex?" the man asked. To illustrate, he held up an invisible tray, then whisked it away.

"Yes," Lowell said with infinite sadness, "I suppose she did."

Eventually, he moved into a one-room flat in Manhattan and stayed in touch with his daughters by phone. He learned after several months that his wife's affair had petered out. (And there was an expression for you.) She tried another, with a police officer. When that didn't pan out, she called Lowell and asked if he wanted to give the marriage another try. Out of pride, Lowell said that was impossible. It had taken him too long to recover from the breakup, if indeed he had recovered at

all. And now, years later, at Gene's restaurant, he sat opposite a
bloated version of the man who had caused him so much pain.

It was a difficult decision, but Lowell decided not to
acknowledge that he recognized Neely and that he was aware of
their history. Why give him the satisfaction? If Neely brought
it up, provoked him, lorded it over him, he would reconsider.
He hadn't entirely ruled out the steak knife.

Lowell steered the conversation into relatively safe areas—
the state of the theatre, the advantages of public transporta-
tion. Should the mayor be permitted to try for a third term?
And all the while, as they ate dinner and chatted perfunctorily,
Lowell's thoughts were divided. On one level, he remained in
the moment. On another, he thought of Sylvia's affair and its
aftermath. At first, he'd kept to himself in his single room. He
had to learn how to make coffee and to deal with his laundry.
Slowly, as if recovering from an illness, he ventured out to a
neighborhood bar and made a few tentative friends. One was
a woman who decorated store windows. She came back to his
apartment and gave him some tips on how to brighten it up.
He learned to cook and was proud of himself for pulling off
a veal roast. Then he bought a car and began to cruise the
nighttime streets in a black Lincoln. Since he was still shy, he
tried drugs for a while, then decided he didn't need them. He
found he was able to meet and attract women when he was
clear-eyed. He moved to a larger apartment and began to give
parties for his new friends and neighbors.

He took care of his family's needs and had plenty of money
to spare. Sailing through the midnight streets in his car, he
often felt like king of the city. One night, to cap it all off, he
met June at a wedding reception. She became the center of his
life. From the moment they met, he lost all interest in other

women. He kept a photograph above his desk in which she has her arms around his neck and looks at him with complete trust and adoration. It was a look he had never seen before. In the photograph, he returns it. They moved in together, were soon married, and had a daughter who could only be described as a love child. Lowell enjoyed every day of his life.

Now, in the restaurant, Lowell could hardly believe he had considered harming the man who sat opposite him. Yet he had that capability. In response to 9/11, he had immediately signed up for an intensive course in martial arts. Suppose there was another attack and Lowell was on an airliner. Why sit around and not try to prevent it? Though he'd lasted only two sessions, he remembered a few moves. Now and then he practiced them. It would take little effort to reach across the table and blind the man. Using the heel of his hand, drive his broad nose back into his brain. And there was always the knife.

But to even *have* these thoughts. To consider injuring an individual who had made possible a glorious new chapter in his life. Neely, McNeely, whatever his name was, might as well have been an angel sent down to compensate for a deceitful marriage. A sullen, prisonlike existence. And Lowell had considered harming him. Breaking his neck. Breaking his back, for that matter. This saint who sat across the table. What kind of person had Lowell become?

"It's still a great restaurant," said Neely as he finished his apple pie.

"Convivial is the feeling I get when I'm here."

"*Convivial*," said Neely with a sigh of pleasure. "What a lovely word."

They made a perfunctory plan to meet again. A bit later, the waiter brought the check. Both men reached for it.

"Let me take that," said the fat man.

"Out of the question," said Lowell, who had gotten to it first. "It's the least I can do."

"That's very kind of you. But you haven't said much about your wife. I saw her at the lake. She's lovely. The kind of person it would be fun to know. Why don't we all get together, me, Eunice, you, and your wife and go up to a restaurant I know of in Castle Hill? You'll like it. I'll rent a limo."

"A *limo?*" said Lowell. "My precious *wife?*"

Thrust back in time, he started for the man.

"You sonofabitch, you should have quit while you were ahead."

THE IMPULSE

*I*n *the years to come, Dwight would ask himself: "What on Earth possessed me to do such a thing?"*

It was so out of character.

Or was it?

He had just left the banquet and was walking along Forty-Sixth Street in a light rain, looking for a car service that was scheduled to pick him up on the southwest corner of the avenue. But perhaps he'd said the southeast corner. He had begun to make that kind of mistake.

Normally, he would have tried to hail a cab. The car service was expensive—he used it only on special occasions. The event he'd attended, a dinner in honor of the publisher who had fired him some months back, fell into that category. There was always the chance that Dwight would be rehired when "things picked up." He'd gotten the invitation, which meant he hadn't been forgotten. Best to show up and stay on the publisher's good side.

As he floundered around looking for the car, an elderly woman appeared at his side. She was breathing heavily, as if it had been an effort to catch up with him. But once she did, the woman, surprisingly, was able to match his pace, step for step.

What he noticed first was her gray, scraggly hair (it had once been blond), her deep—exceptionally deep—wrinkles, her brightly colored designer dress, and her jewelry. The dress had a flamingo pattern that fell just short of being gaudy. It would have blended in nicely at a Palm Beach cocktail party, but not Manhattan in the fall. She wore several necklaces; the most noticeable was a pendant with a giant ruby at its center, encircled by tiny diamonds. Dwight was no expert on precious stones, but he had once been the editor of a coffee-table book on the subject. He would have wagered that the jewelry was worth a fortune. She came across as being scattered. Ditzy.

Had he seen her at the dinner? Possibly. She reminded him of the central character in a play he'd seen as a boy, *The Madwoman of Chaillot*.

As they walked, she stared at him, making him feel uneasy. Elderly people had that effect on him, although, by strict definition, he could be described as elderly himself. He was sixty-eight.

"Do we know each other?" he asked.

They walked together in a matching cadence and might have been mistaken for a couple. Her legs were like sticks.

"Fleming," she said, extending a bony hand. "Antebellum."

Was Fleming her last or first name? As for "antebellum," he guessed that she was conveying something about her lineage. He recalled meeting a novelist from India who told him her name and quickly added: "I'm high-born."

"Dwight," he said, taking her cold bony hand. "Fisher. . . . From the Bronx." He'd been self-conscious about his beginnings in the boroughs, but of late he'd been throwing the facts of his hardscrabble youth around boldly, feeling he had nothing to lose at this point in his life. It might even work to his advantage. Thus far, this new openness hadn't done much for him. He was unemployed, had little in the way of savings, was barely getting by. His prospects were slim. His wife had hung in with him. She loved him, but there were probably limits.

He assumed that he and his unexpected companion had attended the same event.

"Did you enjoy the dinner?"

"Stank," she said.

He feared she was about to hold her nose.

"And the company?"

She pointed a bony thumb downward. This time she did hold her nose.

That's enough of *that*, he thought.

"I guess I'll be moseying along," he said to her. "Pleasure meeting you."

The rain came down a bit harder.

"But what then?" she said vacantly.

He may have been overdramatizing the moment, but he feared that she might sit down in a puddle of rainwater. Jewelry, designer dress, and all. As if she were a patient at some institution. And he would be forced to look at wet granny underwear.

There was a pause while he struggled to respond. Then, in a streak of gallantry or compassion—he was not an unkind man—he said he had a car that should be waiting at the end of the street.

"Perhaps I can give you a lift."

She waved a hand, as if his offer meant nothing to her. Go ahead and desert me, she seemed to say. I'll just stand out in the rain. Or sit in it, for that matter.

He was off the hook but didn't feel that way. She did not seem capable of hailing a cab. How, in any case, would she get one? The street was blocked off by a construction project, which was why he was having all this trouble finding his car. And anyone who's lived in Manhattan knows that the cabs go into hiding at the slightest hint of rain.

Finally, he located the car. The confirmation number was displayed on the windshield, which was a happy circumstance for him. He opened the rear door for his new acquaintance.

"Mmmm," she said, and muttered something that sounded like "gemmumms," a variation, he guessed, of "gentleman."

Was it possible that people in her circle—some Palm Beach circle, or perhaps one in Memphis—addressed one another in baby talk? Wouldn't surprise him a bit.

She lived on the Upper East Side. His apartment was to the extreme West, which was no small issue in terms of logistics and added cost. Still, he'd made the offer and there they were. Dwight adored his wife. His dog. And his flat, if only he could hold on to it. To them. He longed to get home. But for the moment, he felt that he'd been fated to go driving off with this strange elderly woman.

She lived in a compact two-story townhouse. He saw her to the door and stood by to see that she got inside safely. She was surprisingly adept at retrieving the keys in her handbag. He'd expected her to spend a few minutes fumbling around for them and then to drop them on the sidewalk. Or to have left them somewhere. She surprised him by asking if he'd like to come in for a drink.

"There's wine and some milky. I think it's fresh."

The "milky," of course, was distasteful to him. That awful cuteness. Were there people who enjoyed it? Considered it charming? Charleston people came to mind. Perhaps wealthy Charleston people said "milky" to one another. And were awarded points for cleverness.

"I really should be going," he said. And then, unaccountably, he heard himself add, "maybe for just a minute."

Why had he accepted this invitation? Was he looking for a new experience, the nature of which was not clear? At a recent dinner party, one that had run out of gas, the guests had been asked to reveal their favorite word. Dwight's was "adventure." His life had not been filled with derring-do, but there had been a few episodes. He'd been a POW at the tail end of the Korean War. And there had been a two-week period of madness with a Senegalese actress in Santa Monica. Neither of them wore a stitch for the length of the romance. But his was not a long list of daring adventures. He joked to his wife that, at this point in life, his idea of a wild night was a Szechuan dinner and a low-budget movie.

Yet here he was accepting the invitation of a somewhat daft octogenarian (she might have been ninety) to join her for a drink in her townhouse apartment. Did he see it as an adventure? Or was there some other motive? He had no idea at the moment.

Further along, he might realize that he had always known what he had in mind. But not just then.

"Oh, good," she said, once he'd accepted her invitation. "Drinkies."

There it was again. The cuteness. And it was Palm Beach. He was sure of it now. Wealthy Palm Beach people in all their baby-talking cuteness. How Noël Coward would have adored them. Or so they felt.

The interior of the first floor—he never got to see the second— surprised him. Somehow he'd expected a garish décor—a Halloween theme, or perhaps a collection of dolls, eerily lining the walls. A parrot in a cage. A wooden horse from an old merry-go-round. What he discovered instead was a large and handsomely appointed living room with an immaculate *Town & Country* feel to it. How he loved to be wrong. The furnishings were spare, but each piece would appear to have been selected with great care. "Tasteful" did not do justice to the look of it. A designer and perhaps a collector had been at work here. And there was no way the woman could have maintained the place on her own. There had to be servants who had been given the night off.

There were more than a few photographs mounted on the wall of a short, portly gentleman with a neatly trimmed beard, holding the reins of a horse, a prize-winner, garlanded with a floral wreath. In other photographs, he stood beside a giant fish, a marlin, or perhaps a tuna, on a dock in Key West, or some such location. The fish looked to have been a trophy. Perhaps the man had nosed out Hemingway in a competition. Dwight had the feeling that the dapper little man was no longer on the planet, though his money had stayed behind.

The woman, Fleming—he still wasn't sure if this was a surname—more or less confirmed the demise of the gentleman in the photographs.

"Mr. Barnes," she said to Dwight. "Poor Mr. Barnes."

Then, staying in character, she put her hand to her midsection and said: "Tummy."

She tiptoed into a kitchen, high-tech in design, opened the refrigerator, and sniffed at a container of milk. "Eeeuww," she said, putting it back quickly and making Dwight wonder again what he was doing in this apartment. As if sensing she was about to lose him, she switched to a normal conversational style.

"Would you care for a glass of wine?"

"I'd like that," said Dwight, cautiously accepting her offer.

He noticed her manner of speech kept altering, going from the bizarre to the simple and straightforward—as it suited her.

He sat on a couch and tried the wine, which wasn't half bad, considering it had come from a bottle that had been opened perhaps days before. Months? She poured a glass for herself, sipped it, and sat primly beside him. Then she leaned in close and said: "How's about a li'l ol' blowjob?"

Good *Christ*, he said to himself in horror.

And then, blandly, he said aloud, "I don't believe so."

He did not, it should be pointed out, have a long history of turning down such invitations. Then he added, idiotically, but perhaps to show good manners, "Not just now."

"We could clean you up and flip you over on your bell," she said.

Then she looked off languorously with her gorgeous blue eyes.

"Mr. Barnes trained me in the technique. He said a gentleman enjoys it."

"I'm sure a gentleman does," said Dwight, outwardly unflappable. "And Mr. Barnes must have been quite a chap."

Chap? Had he said chap? Where had that come from? Bertie Wooster? Though he was a fanatic when it came to British satire, the Wodehouse novels were not among his favorites. (This puzzled—and annoyed—his friends.)

Perhaps he had channeled Mr. Barnes's verbal style. Or there may have been a class struggle in play. The woman, in all her confusion, with an elegant past. The boy from the Bronx reaching up to a higher social tier.

With gnarled and bejeweled fingers, she reached for his crotch. He countered—was this a counter?—by snatching the ruby-centered pendant from her neck.

"Ooooh," she said, rubbing her neck. "That hurt."

She rubbed it some more.

"Boo-boo," she said. "Kiss boo-boo."

"Hold on a second," he said, dropping the necklace into his jacket pocket. There was no way he was going to kiss a turkey neck. He found a washcloth on the kitchen counter and ran some water over it. Then he returned to the couch and gently rubbed the reddened part of her neck. When she covered his hand with hers, in gratitude, he held her wrist and yanked a huge diamond ring from her big knuckled finger. He slipped it into his pocket beside the necklace.

"Oooooh," she said again, rubbing her finger this time. "*Big* boo-boo. Hurt suppin' awful."

"I'm sure it does," he said without thought.

Using the same cloth, he rubbed the finger gently and got to his feet.

"It's nothing serious. I should be going."

"Ooooh," she repeated, then got to her feet and looked at her reflection in a wall mirror. "And my *maquillage*," she said, in horror, ignoring her injuries for the moment. "Just *look* at me."

"You look fine," he said, wondering where he'd heard the term *maquillage* before. Must have been years back. Some fashion person in the Hamptons.

"You'll feel better in the morning," he said as he edged slowly toward the door.

"I don't give a fuck," she said, stamping her foot.

"Well, you *should*," he said mindlessly.

And then he was gone. He searched for a cab. With remarkable ease, he found one. When he had settled into the darkness of the backseat, he reached into his pocket to feel the jewelry and to make sure he hadn't been daydreaming.

As the cab entered Central Park, his heart began to flutter and he could feel his pulse rising. And why was there all that heat behind his neck. His physician had mentioned that a pacemaker might be a good idea—when Dwight felt up to it. Does anyone ever "feel up to" a pacemaker? He had conveniently forgotten the conversation. Not that there was any right moment, but this was no time to have a heart attack.

What had gotten into him? What had *possessed* him to do such a thing? "Possessed" was the right word too. Did he have his eye on the jewelry the moment he saw her on the street? Possibly. And now that he had the swag, what would he do with it? Where did "swag" come from? Did they still *have* swag? Or did it disappear with old Warner Bros. movies? And weren't you supposed to have a "fence" for a situation like this? Someone to convert the stolen goods—the swag—into cash? Where would he find one? Did they still have them? A fence? He could not think of a single person he could call and ask, "Do you know of a good fence?" Or even a bad one.

The Diamond District was a possibility. He imagined a Hasidic individual—cherry-red lips in a snow-white beard—with a glass magnifier affixed to his eye. Squinting at the jewelry—the swag—and evaluating its worth. The ruby pendant would be of particular interest. With a sigh, as if it was a nuisance to bother with such trifles, he would say that rubies were not much in demand these days (a lie). Sensing, *knowing*, that the jewelry had been stolen, he would then quote a price that was no doubt a tenth of its actual worth. Dwight, nervous, close to panic, probably a first-timer, would be happy to gobble up whatever crumbs were offered to him.

But wouldn't there be papers to be signed? Traceable

papers? And security cameras? Unless Dwight fled to Uruguay, or someplace like that—it did cross his mind—he'd be a sitting duck for the police.

As the car approached Riverside Drive, his behavior, his act of madness, continued to nag at him. The central character in a novel he'd enjoyed was asked why he was about to run off with a friend's wife. *"Because I can,"* came his answer. That made literary sense, but it wasn't useful to Dwight as a practical matter. He hadn't taken the jewelry because it was *possible.* He was sure of that. Then what was it? He was on shaky financial ground, but a sudden jewelry heist, and it barely qualified as a heist, wasn't going to bail him out. Especially when he had to fork over a large slice of it to a fence. Or a diamond dealer. Six months' rent would be about the size of it. Unless he'd underestimated the value of the two pieces. In any case, he would soon be off to federal detention.

Dwight did have what he himself described, amusingly, as a mild case of Tourette's syndrome. But was it all that mild? At a literary award ceremony, he'd heard himself ask a distinguished Polish poet, a future Nobelist, if he knew of a restaurant that served great pierogies. On another occasion, he'd been assigned to accompany a visiting school administrator around the city. On the steps of the New York Public Library, he yielded to a compulsion and asked the middle-aged woman what kind of underwear she had on. The term "brain fart" had come into much-too-common use at the time. Dismissing Dwight's remarks as falling into that category, she smiled thinly, then continued along with their discussion of Byzantine architecture. Caught up in a celebratory moment at a cocktail party, Dwight had lifted his publisher—a small man—off the ground and danced him around the room as if he were a tango partner. Though the man seemed to accept all of this with equanimity, there was a chance that the episode had led to Dwight's dismissal. Now that he thought about the incident, it *had* led to his dismissal.

At no point that he could remember did Dwight *want* the jewelry. He certainly didn't want it at the moment. He could have returned it, but the prospect of facing the woman and her *maquillage* at two in the morning was daunting. He could, of course, just throw it out the window. Or simply hand it over to the driver—a Bangladeshi.

"Here," he could say, "do what you want with it. Maybe your wife would like it."

Once again, the theft would be traceable back to him. And why enrich a strange Bangladeshi, who probably did have a fence? A Bangladeshi fence.

As they approached his building Dwight tried to pull himself together. He was fairly certain his wife would still be awake. His treasured wife. The therapist. The calm, sensible one. She knew him. Again and again she'd seen him through choppy waters. The tango episode that had cost him his job. Scraping up every dime they had to invest in a Canadian start-up that had gone belly-up within a month. (The two crisp young executives had been entirely convincing on the financial channel.) Then putting a few dimes together and making another blunder with a chain of Midwestern furniture stores. Turning down the lucrative directorship of a London publishing conglomerate because the personnel manager had made a remark about his thinning hair. She had suffered through all of that and more—and stuck with him.

As soon as she got the drift of it, she would know exactly

what to do. And she would draw up a sensible and conservative plan. One that would keep him out of prison.

He turned the key in the lock. The dog, a Havanese, came running up to him, ready to forgive him anything. Much like Hitler's dog Blondi, who licked the Führer's face after he'd ravaged Czechoslovakia.

His wife sat calmly next to the fireplace, reading one of her beloved mysteries. The very sight of her erased his anxiety. He was home. Safe. The cleaning woman had been in. The place was immaculate. It wasn't his, but there was no reason he couldn't enjoy the remaining nine months on the lease. He'd probably made too much of the night's episode. It had been a mistake to take the jewelry. But who on Earth goes through life without making a blunder or two? Half a dozen in his case. No great harm had been done. Chances are the woman, in her state, had already forgotten what had happened. And wouldn't miss the ring and necklace. No doubt she had buckets full of the stuff. Full of precious stones. More than likely she was wondering what she had done with her bedroom slippers. And concerned about her ridiculous maquillage.

He'd get a good night's sleep. No point in telling his wife about the theft. Was there any need in a marriage, a good marriage, to fill out a report on every breath you took? He'd see it all clearly in the morning. He was beginning to see it clearly now. There were any number of options. He could keep the jewelry. Flush it. Sell it somehow and be done with it. Put it away somewhere and worry about it later. Even mail it, as if a Samaritan had found it on the street, just outside her front door.

His wife was totally caught up in her mystery novel. He kissed her forehead so as not to disturb her.

"Hi, darling," she said. "Before I forget, there's a detective who called and wanted to have a chat with you. . . . Do you know a woman named Fleming?"

THE PEACE PROCESS

a novella

PART ONE

1990

From his reasonably comfortable room in the King David Hotel, William Kleiner looked out on the old walled city of Jerusalem and tried without success to love Israel. It's true that he had only been in the country for a few hours, but his first impressions were not encouraging. At JFK, when he'd told the security guard that he was in the movie business, her nose had twisted to the side as if she'd smelled rotten fish. Then she'd questioned him for hours. Who gave him the ticket? Why Kleiner and not somebody else? How long had he had it and did he keep it in his suit jacket when he went to restaurants? Did he happen to be a Frequent Flyer? Kleiner understood the sensitive security needs of the beleaguered state, but was it necessary for them to know that his second cousin's name was Dworkin? Why, the woman needed to know, did his mother get out of the stocking business on Hester Street?

He was tempted to tell them to forget it—in Japan, they could hardly *wait* to let him into the country—but the truth is, he needed his current assignment. Once a respected film director, his career had gone into the toilet after a string of turkeys. He was now officially considered burned out. He had been lucky to land a job as a location scout for a picture that had been described to backers as a Jewish *Star Wars*.

Finally, as if they were doing him a favor, he was allowed to board the plane. The intifada was at its height. As a result, there weren't many passengers on the flight. He introduced himself to a slim, well-dressed man in Business Class who said he was employed by a think tank in Haifa. Kleiner saw in the man a compatible soul. Delighted by his good fortune, he prepared himself for a stimulating transatlantic conversation.

"I'd love to hear about your work."

"And I'd love to tell you about it, but unfortunately my plan is to do a little thinking."

Graciously, the man recommended a few good restaurants in Jerusalem, then turned away, thoughtfully holding his chin in one hand.

Disappointed, Kleiner settled in and watched *Misery*, the only selection, and a film he felt he'd had the skills to direct, if only they had given him a shot at it.

After a huge dinner and a successful nap, he found himself staring at the flight attendant and realized the man reminded him of Gil Fleugel, a friend who had committed suicide. The man had Fleugel's hairline, the same powerful trunk, an identical smile. A charming individual, Fleugel throughout his life had sought out and enjoyed the company of celebrities, although it weighed on him that he himself, a shoe salesman, had never done anything noteworthy. When he realized he never would, he took a car off a cliff in Locust Valley, Long Island, leaving instructions that he be cremated. Kleiner attended his funeral. Speaker after speaker admitted they didn't know what to make of the man. Even the rabbi threw up his hands. Was it possible Fleugel had faked his death and tied on with El Al?

Throughout the flight, Kleiner watched the attendant

serve treats and collect trays, bringing his knees together and dipping his legs in a style reminiscent of Fleugel as a host at cocktail parties. When the plane touched down at Ben Gurion Airport, Kleiner could contain himself no longer.

"Fleugel," he cried out. "I know it's you. Tell me I'm not mistaken, for Christ's sakes."

In response to the blasphemy, the think tank man shouted "shame" and a rabbi beat his breast and davened. The attendant flashed a winsome smile as the doors flew open on the Holy Land.

The first thing Kleiner saw when he left the plane was a long line of Mercedes cars, as far as the eye could see. At the height of his career, when he was able to afford the German luxury car, Kleiner had shown solidarity with the Jews and stuck with a Cadillac. Had he known that Israel was virtually a huge Mercedes dealership, he might have done otherwise. Now it was too late. He was lucky to own a Saab.

The driver he selected was a stocky man with butcher's arms and a forest of black curly hair. He told Kleiner he was from Poland and worked seven days a week to support his wife and five children. Even though they were fully grown, they continued to live in his tiny flat. It was a harsh life, relieved only by an excellent medical plan and the kindness of an occasional passenger from America who remembered him each Chanukkah with a gift in cash.

"Here's how to reach me," he said, handing Kleiner a card with his name and address.

Kleiner was offended by the driver's lack of subtlety, but he put the card in his wallet anyway. Who knows, if his career took off, maybe he'd send the man a few dollars.

As they approached the city, Kleiner looked out on the barren desert and wondered why he wasn't moved. It was his first trip to Israel; he'd expected to be overcome with emotion. Years back, he had spotted an El Al airliner taxiing through the fog at LaGuardia and had begun to cry uncontrollably. Was it only Jewish airplanes that moved him? The thought was absurd. Once he settled in at the hotel and mingled with a few Jews, he felt confident he'd start to cry again.

When the cab pulled up at the hotel, Kleiner, mindful of the driver's straitened circumstances, overtipped him, then said he'd been thinking over the man's situation.

"Maybe you should tell the children to move out."

"And waste my breath," the man said bitterly.

He flung Kleiner's valise to the ground and drove off.

Wearily, Kleiner picked up his luggage and wondered what prompted him to get involved in other people's affairs. Possibly it was because a psychiatrist he had been seeing on and off for many years had recently dropped dead, and this was Kleiner's way of continuing the man's practice.

After he had checked into the hotel, Kleiner approached the concierge, an elderly Viennese who gave the impression of having tired feet.

"Can you recommend a restaurant? It's my first trip to Israel and I don't know my way around."

"What took you so long to get here? You're no spring chicken."

Kleiner ignored the gratuitous comment about his age. He cited the example of his cousin Gloria who had labored long and hard for Israel, organizing theatre parties for the B'nai Brith on a noncommission basis.

"And she hasn't been here either."

"Scribble down her number," said the concierge. "We're

coming to New York in August. My wife is dying to see *The Lion King*."

The concierge pointed out that Kleiner had arrived on the Sabbath. The city was locked up tight as a drum. His best bet was to eat a kosher dinner in the hotel dining room.

"That's if I can get you in."

After Kleiner had slipped the man a few dollars, the concierge led him into the dining room, seating him next to a hollow-eyed Frenchman, the only other single. The man extended a weak hand. Recently widowed, he had bought a condo in Tel Aviv.

"Away from France," he said, his voice cracking, "maybe I can forget my poor wife."

Over a five-course dinner, he described in detail her valiant but ultimately losing battle with illness.

"What did she die of?" asked Kleiner, who had barely touched his gefilte fish.

"Cancer," the man said with a loud, mournful wail, causing a table of six to whip their heads around.

Kleiner had never before heard such a tragic-sounding utterance, possibly because of the French accent. He had thought it might be nice to get to know the man and possibly receive an invitation to his condo. But he could see it was much too early in the mourning period for a friendship to take hold. Kleiner got to his feet, patted the man on the shoulder, and said he hoped he would find a little happiness in the years to come.

"You won't stay for the noodle pudding?" said the man, wiping away a tear.

"Some other time."

Emma. Green eyes. The twinkle. The unconscionably pretty body. Kleiner? Dead in the water. And that was the start of it.

. . .

Kleiner walked outside and took a seat on the patio. The only other guests were a pair of Hasids who discussed ice-cream franchises in the moonlight. When Kleiner lit a cigar, one of them jumped to his feet.

"Put that out," he said, wagging a long finger. "Don't you know it's the Sabbath?"

"Forgive me," said Kleiner, stubbing out the cigar in an ashtray and graciously accepting the two-and-a-half-dollar loss. A fly-by-night Jew, it had been years since he had set foot in a synagogue. Yet he had no wish to offend the devout, especially in Israel.

Excusing himself, he walked back toward the lobby.

"And don't try it in the room," the first Hasid called out to him.

"Because we'll know," said his friend.

In the lobby, Kleiner considered taking a cab to the more cosmopolitan Tel Aviv for a few quick puffs. Would the men follow him there? Rather than chance it, he returned to his room where everything from the old-fashioned radio to the shower curtain reminded him of his childhood apartment in Washington Heights; this would have been comforting, except that the loved ones who had surrounded him as a boy were dead and buried. This included the cleaning lady, who had reserved a plot right next to his parents.

Standing on the small balcony, he heard a voice cry out in the night and thought it might be the Frenchman about to go off the roof. Then he realized it was a muezzin, summoning the faithful to prayer. Kleiner wouldn't have minded doing a little praying himself. But what would he pray for? Another wife to drive him crazy? His next hard-on? Peace on Earth was an obvious choice. But what he really wanted was another chance at the spotlight so that he could show his face in top restaurants.

His mood was sorrowful, which was puzzling since he hadn't even visited his first Holocaust memorial. Music had always lifted his spirits, so he turned on the radio, hoping to pick up a few joyous songs from the Negev. All he got were cricket scores from Sri Lanka.

Then he realized he was not alone. A young man in a black suit was setting up a tray beside his bed. The suit was four sizes too big for him. When he turned toward Kleiner, his lips were wet and his eyes unfocused, as if he had been hit on the head a few times.

"Your tea, sir," said the man. "Just the way you like it."

"I don't like tea," said Kleiner. "And how did you get in here?"

"I don't want to disturb you," said the man, not quite answering the question. "May I get you some figs?"

"That won't be necessary," said Kleiner, although, if the truth were told, figs were a favorite of his.

"I'll make sure there are no worms in them."

"Even so," said Kleiner, "I'd like my privacy."

"As you wish, sir. But maybe you can explain something to me. My brother is getting married for the second time in Queens. Every time I ask the authorities if I can go to the wedding, they tell me to go and fuck myself.

"Why is that, Mr. Kleiner?" he asked, the voice of equanimity.

"I'm sure they have their reasons."

"You're an important man, sir," he continued. "You have powerful friends. Maybe you can help me."

"I'm not so important these days," said Kleiner, implying of course that he once was.

"Kamal is my only brother," said the man, near tears. "Soon he'll be married and I won't be there. If I were a Jew, I'd be on the plane, but because I'm a *farshtunkene* Arab, they laugh at me."

Increasingly agitated, he fell to his knees. With his arms pressed to his chest, like Jolson at the Winter Garden, he cried out, "*Help me get to LeFrak City!*"

Despite the man's passionate appeal, Kleiner was strangely unmoved by his story. What was so important about a wedding, especially these days, when most marriages ended in divorce anyway? He conceded that Arab marriages might be more long-standing, but nonetheless, his heart remained unbroken. Maybe if the brother needed a kidney, Kleiner would be inclined to pick up the phone. But even then, who would he call, the prime minister? The busy head of state would laugh in his face.

"I can't help you," said Kleiner. "I just got here and I've got a full plate."

"You don't understand," said the man, the color draining from his face. "The psychology here. It's killing me."

Gasping for air, he ran around the room, holding his temples as if there were electrodes attached. At the moment, Kleiner felt the Arab was capable of doing anything. This included stabbing Kleiner in the heart with a bread knife, a poor start to his trip. Maybe he should call security. But there was no point in having the man dismissed, which would only add to his troubles, possibly putting him on the unemployment line with newly arrived Russians.

Kleiner stepped in front of the Arab and put an arm around his shoulders.

"It's late," he said, gently steering him into the corridor. "We both could use some sleep."

The last statement was patently untrue, since the man, despite his unfocused eyes, appeared to be well rested.

Kleiner shut the door and double-locked it. Despite the precaution, he didn't feel safe. The Arab had gotten in before; he could get in again. It's possible he had a key.

Trying to compose himself, Kleiner wondered if there had been a case for helping the man. As far as Kleiner could tell, he was an Israeli Arab, with the same rights and privileges as any citizen, except possibly the important ones. Kleiner was no expert in Israeli civic affairs, but he had read this much in a dentist's office, possibly in *GQ*.

What harm could come from letting the man travel to Queens, especially if he promised to come back in a few weeks and not make any side trips to missile silos?

Still, the Israelis were wise. Possibly they suspected him of having ties to Syria and were keeping an eye on him. But if this were true, why would they let him run loose in a top hotel, with access not only to Kleiner but to visiting rock stars?

What bothered Kleiner the most was that he may not have shown sufficient compassion. This was a touchy point. Pleading involvement with his work, he had always been a little distant to friends and loved ones. But he had a clean slate when it came to helping strangers. Rare was the appeal from a charity that went unanswered in the Kleiner household of one, especially the blind ones. Only recently he had fired off a check to a new group that helped gay men who felt terrible that they didn't have AIDS yet. Then too, in Central Park, he had disarmed a souvlaki salesman who was about to stab his cousin over a minor theft. (Fortunately, Kleiner's heroism had been observed by a passing commodities broker who whispered, "Well done.")

Was this the picture of a selfish man?

Nonetheless, he remained disturbed by the incident. Thousands of miles from home, he felt naked and alone. The fact that there were Jews all over the place was of little comfort since he didn't know any of them. Ironically, in Japan, where the stores were crowded with anti-Semitic bestsellers, he'd felt warm and cozy in his hotel room. Maybe in the formerly Nazi Germany he would find total peace and security.

Kleiner felt like calling someone, but his contacts in Israel were minimal. His accountant had given him the name of a great beauty who had been the mistress of several of the country's founding fathers. But the woman was well along in her seventies. Should he ask her to hobble over with a cane and keep him company? His contact in the film industry lived way out in the desert. There was no need to disturb the man at an ungodly hour. A call to Emma, his estranged wife, was a possibility. She had a great and compassionate heart, but unfortunately she was addicted to everything; this included salt and pepper and the air they breathed. Unwilling to see her destroy a fine mind by eating Mounds bars and watching daytime soaps, Kleiner, like a thief in the night, had slipped out of her life. He resisted calling her for fear that she would develop a few new addictions while they were on the phone.

There were stray friends he could ring up in the States, but in truth he was afraid of the time differential. That someone could be eating lunch at one end of the phone while Kleiner prepared for bed at the other drove him close to insanity, as did all concepts of time. He'd once read one page of an Einstein biography and had to lie down with a headache.

So he decided to tough it out and prepare for bed. He looked in the mirror and saw one of those attractive bald men, or at least that's what he had been told on those occasions when his weight was under control. He had brown eyes, a straight nose, and wonderful teeth, which he had inherited from his father, along with the ability to take naps at a moment's notice. He was not quite six feet tall, which had always annoyed him. Either you're six feet tall or you're not. If you're close, don't bother me.

After a quick sponge bath, Kleiner checked the door again and dressed for bed, feeling vulnerable in his shortie night-gown. The second his head hit the pillow, the walls of the room shook from the sonic boom of an Israeli Mirage. As if in response, prayer floated up from the walled city. Then the phone rang, causing his heart to pound, even though he had recently passed a stress test with flying colors.

He picked up the receiver cautiously.

"Yes?"

"This is Mahmoud," said the familiar voice at the other end. "I thought you might want some halvah."

Kleiner flew out of bed the next morning, all thoughts of the troubling incident erased from his mind. If there were an award for making fresh starts in the morning, Kleiner would win it, hands down. He dressed quickly and enthusiastically—after all, there was a whole new country out there, full of surprises. It would be hours before he had a chance to feel miserable again.

Kleiner plunged into the lobby. It was filled with women from New Jersey, making preparations to visit historical and religious sites, and also lining up poolside cabanas. As he grew older, Kleiner increasingly sought out the company of Jews. Once he was actually among them, however, he wasn't one hundred percent sure he was enjoying himself. Since he was uneasy in the company of gentiles too, what did that mean? That he was only happy around studio executives?

On a couch, in a corner of the lobby, the sad young Frenchman held hands with an attractive woman. She had shoulder-length black hair and long graceful legs. Kleiner marveled at the man's ability to attract such a lovely creature so soon after his loss. With no tragedy to his credit, Kleiner was unable to do the same.

The Frenchman waved over Kleiner and introduced his friend, Naomi Glickstein, a teacher of junior high who lived in midtown Manhattan.

Eyes glued to the Frenchman, the woman extended a snow-white hand.

"My pleasure."

"Look," said the Frenchman, as if Kleiner were about to judge him. "It was a terrible thing I went through. But what should I do, kill myself?"

"You have to go on," said Kleiner supportively.

"I told him the same thing," said Naomi.

The Frenchman nodded, then groaned sorrowfully, raining kisses on the woman's arm.

Sick with envy, Kleiner excused himself and headed for the dining room.

There he was confronted by a sea of breakfast delicacies, chief among them smoked and pickled fish of a hundred different varieties. It was a dream come true for Kleiner, who quickly grabbed a plate. With his mouth watering, he approached the display. But after circling the banquet several times, he was unable to make a choice and settled for a slice of grapefruit and some cornflakes, for his health.

After breakfast, he took a seat in the lobby and checked the

Jerusalem Post, to see if by some wild coincidence one of his old movies had finally made it to the Middle East.

When he next looked up, he saw a tall, handsome fellow in denim shorts and hiking shoes come bounding across the lobby toward him, the man's legs exploding with vitality. He introduced himself as Hilly, a veteran of four wars and currently with the film office.

"Are you ready to go?" he asked in the booming voice of a tank commander.

"As ready as I'll ever be," said Kleiner.

He was exhausted just looking at the man.

"It's important to get one thing straight," said Hilly as they headed for the hotel entrance. "I can't show you Yankee Stadium or the Stork Club or Radio City Music Hall. And if you're expecting an introduction to Mickey Rooney or Cher, you've come to the wrong place."

Kleiner took note of the man's scrambled and time-warped vision of American culture. He gave what he felt was the expected reply.

"That's not why I'm here."

"Good," said Hilly as they left the hotel. "Because I can show you something that in my opinion is much more important."

"And that is . . . ?"

"History."

He pointed to a ditch beside the road that was covered by an iron grate.

"Look down there, for example."

Kleiner peered inside and saw a dark hole, nothing more.

"Right below you," said Hilly, "Roman centurions played cards two thousand years ago. What do you think?"

Kleiner said it was fascinating, but that he didn't think he could fit a camera crew into such a narrow space.

"You can't?" said Hilly, clearly disappointed. "Oh, well, don't worry. There's more, much more. We're not finished by a long shot."

After a short walk, they reached the Walled City and entered through the Jaffa Gate. Goats brushed against Kleiner, as did weaving camels and Bedouin women with bowls on their heads. Bearded Coptics pushed their way past blind Ethiopians who leaned on biblical staffs and stared at the sun. His head swimming, Kleiner threw up his hands, as if to protect himself from a shower of history. A black man in a Saints jacket reached out to steady him.

"I'm St. Germain from New Orleans. My hand and my heart."

Kleiner thanked the man for assisting him, then joined Hilly, who seemed to be enjoying his disassociated state.

"You see that," he said. "And you thought Forty-Second Street was hot shit."

They entered the Arab Quarter and were quickly swept up in a stream of shopkeepers who had closed for the day out of respect for the intifada. Sullen men in kaffiyehs pressed in upon Kleiner; though there wasn't a peep out of them, he had never before felt such quiet rage. Hilly, seemingly impervious to their hostility, strolled along in a carefree manner, whistling a tune from *Fiddler*. Kleiner thought he saw the gleam of a knife.

"Just out of curiosity, do you carry a weapon?"

"I can't answer that because of security reasons. But I can tell you this. These people are happy, if only they would relax a little and stop worrying so much. We're completely safe."

Unconvinced, Kleiner was relieved when Hilly led them

away from the crowd; with Kleiner following, the Israeli mounted a narrow flight of stairs to the rooftop of the Arab marketplace. All Jerusalem stretched out before them. Kleiner nodded sagely as Hilly ticked off its wonders—the Mount of Olives, the Garden of Gethsemane, Mount Scopus, and a cluster of new condos on a hill. Kleiner was embarrassed by his thin knowledge of biblical times. He had some small expertise on Hammurabi and recalled that the ancient Jews had invented the Right of First Refusal, later to be refined by contract negotiators at Warner Bros. History in general ran through Kleiner like a sieve. He knew of Lenin's self-consciousness about his sparse hair, Bazin's curiously effeminate manner of sitting a horse, and Gallieni's prostate condition as he valiantly defended Paris in the Great War. But not much more.

Kleiner wondered about the Mount of Olives cemetery. As of yet, he'd made no arrangements for his own burial, although he was leaning toward a plot beside his beloved parents and the cleaning lady. Another possibility was that he be laid to rest with other location scouts.

Correctly reading his thoughts, Hilly told him to forget about the ancient burial ground. It was felt that the Messiah would walk through it on his approach to Jerusalem; therefore the site was reserved for high-ranking dignitaries and an occasional blue-jeans manufacturer.

"It would cost you at least fifty thousand to be buried there."

A few feet away, a sharp-featured man in a fedora overheard them. He looked up from his guidebook and handed Kleiner a card.

"I can get you in for twenty-five," he said.

He tipped his hat and slipped away.

Kleiner pocketed the card. Who knows, if he made a score, it might come in handy.

After a respectful trip to the Western Wall, the two men returned to Kleiner's hotel, passing a lone vendor along the way.

Kleiner stopped to look at a goatskin credit-card holder, then put it back when Hilly insisted the price was exorbitant.

When the two men walked off, the vendor cried out after them.

"Go ahead, my friend. Take him to buy from a Jew. But be careful. When night falls, don't turn your back."

Though the words were chilling, the cadence was appealing. Kleiner wondered momentarily if, with a little shaping, they could form the basis of a Levantine rock lyric, the vendor, of course, to be compensated. The man's voice, its commercial use notwithstanding, followed Kleiner back to the hotel. It reminded him that his first order of business was to see to it that his own Arab, the troubled man from room service, wasn't lying in wait for him.

When he was reasonably sure this wasn't the case, Kleiner lay down on the bed and allowed himself to wonder what it would be like to live in Jerusalem and never again feel the sting of anti-Semitism. Only weeks before, at a bar in Brooklyn Heights, he had been accosted by a sheetrock salesman who said you had to be a Jew to direct a movie. Kleiner had fired back with the examples of Preston Sturges and John Ford, receiving the support of several cineastes at the bar. But the man was unpersuaded. The attack rankled.

Kleiner's own wife had been called a kike at a posh Connecticut reception, despite the fact that she was a practicing

Catholic. Kleiner, of course, defended her with a quick fist-fight that brought down an otherwise wonderful evening.

All of this would be unthinkable in the Holy Land.

He had few ties to the States—a fading career, a paper-thin marriage, a cousin who made irritating calls to see if he had anything on the fire. Employment in Israel might be a problem—he would never take a job away from a Russian. But most were violinists. How many location scouts could there be among them? Still, a move would mean a farewell to Scotty Pippin, not to mention Dan Rather, Puerto Ricans, and Kevin Spacey. It's true that the Carnegie Delicatessen wasn't what it once was—but there was still Shun Lee East, Gallaghers, and Joe Allen, not to mention Spago on the West Coast, if they would still let him in. Without getting into his deeper ties to the founding fathers, his hero Grant, and the Hudson Bay Company, he could see that a move to the Holy Land would be premature at the moment. He decided not to send for his files in New York.

Kleiner had dinner in his room. Then, as if he wasn't lonely enough, he walked out on the bleak terrace for a look at the stars. There, standing in the moonlight, was Naomi Glickstein, dressed in a tailored suit and high heels, as if for a convention.

A product of the old school, Kleiner raised his hand to his hat, even though he wasn't wearing one.

"Good evening."

"Oh, hi," said Naomi, fanning her large bosom. "I just came out for some air. It's like a steam bath in that lobby. For a second, I thought I would *plotz*."

The harsh Yiddish word was jarring to Kleiner's ear. Yet at the same time, he found it oddly stimulating, perhaps because it had been spoken so unexpectedly by an attractive contemporary person. He felt what he could only describe as a frisson. Kleiner had read about the sensation in connection with the novels of Stendhal and had always wanted to experience one. It may have been his first frisson. He joined her on the patio below.

"Are you enjoying your stay in Israel?" he asked.

"I was until I met that *meshuggeneh* Frenchman. The man buried his wife two minutes ago and already he's hot to trot."

"He just wants to get back on the horse," said Kleiner, attracted of course to the woman and aware that he may have been undermining his own position.

"Let him find another customer. I have my own *mishegoss*."

Though Kleiner didn't press her for details, Naomi volunteered that she had just ended a six-month affair with a famed urologist who had been a consultant on more than one hundred thousand penises.

"I'm sure you've heard of him. Sol Brown."

"The name is vaguely familiar. Doesn't he write novels?"

"No, no, that's Dan Brown. Sol is strictly penises."

"Don't misunderstand," she said sadly. "Sol is a lovely man and we had six beautiful months. The sex, dare I say, was mindblowing. But it turned out he was married and neglected to mention it."

"Maybe he forgot," said Kleiner, attempting a limp defense of the renowned specialist.

"Maybe I'm a *shiksa*," said Naomi, with a rueful chuckle.

"That you're not," said Kleiner, drawing a sharp look.

Nonetheless, she hooked her arm through his and said, "Come, let's take a walk. It'll do us both good."

Kleiner appreciated the physical contact, although he quickly realized that she may have been holding on to him to keep from stumbling in her high heels. In truth, she was a little clumsy, and this, too, he found strangely appealing. After years of being attracted to graceful women, he now found himself drawn to klutzes, evidence perhaps of an enlarged humanity.

"What's it like to teach junior high?" he asked, although he had little interest in the subject. (While he couldn't deny the importance of molding young minds, he preferred to be spared the details.)

"If you could teach, it would be fine. But all they do is try to look up my dress. Then they leave notes on my desk with such *schmutz* that even Sol himself was embarrassed when he read them."

Kleiner sympathized with her. But he also felt a measure of understanding for the tortured adolescents, trying to concentrate on social science in the disconcerting presence of their sensuous teacher.

"Maybe if you were homely, they would learn."

"Thank you, kind sir. And flattery will get you everywhere."

It was a tired remark, repeated a thousand times at singles bars, but Kleiner enjoyed it all the same. Why shouldn't he have a little innocuous repartee in his life? Where was it written that he had to restrict his conversation to Spinoza and the mysteries of the cosmos?

They stopped at a garden beside the pool, where the air was sweet and aromatic, possibly enriched by the clean gardenia fragrance that came from the direction of Naomi's shoulders.

"May I ask what your work is?" she said. "That is, if I'm not meddling."

"Not at all," said Kleiner.

He told her that he was in the movie business, not bothering to point out that he was hanging on by his thumbs as a lowly location scout.

"May I read you a little something of mine?" she asked.

"Please," said Kleiner, praying it wasn't a screenplay.

Rummaging around in her purse, she produced what appeared to be a rolled-up piece of parchment, delicately tied with a pink ribbon. Unfurling it, she put on a pair of horn-rimmed glasses and began to read:

> *When I look at*
> *the moon and the stars*
> *I could burst*

> *When I contemplate*
> *the soul and the universe*
> *I could burst*

> *Sometimes I think*
> *of the Hereafter*
> *and the Here and Now*
> *as well*
> *and I could burst*

The poem went on to describe all the considerations that could cause the narrator to burst—war, hunger in Darfur, the deficit, the population explosion, unfair hiring practices, the plight of the Tamil minority in Sri Lanka—all of it leading to a final verse, for the recitation of which Naomi removed her glasses and addressed the heavens:

> *But most of all, my darling*
> *When I think of your humane face*
> *THEN I COULD REALLY BURST.*

Kleiner had some quibbles with the text and certain aspects of the construction. But he was not about to deny the sincerity and conviction that had gone into its creation.

"It's lovely."

Naomi lowered her eyes.

"Thank you. Sol liked it too, but it means more coming from a professional. I plan to call it 'I Could Burst.'"

"You almost have to," said Kleiner.

Both realized the hour was late. Kleiner walked Naomi back to the lobby. A sexual lunatic in the '70s, he now practiced a more decorous style, no doubt in response to the turbulent climate of the previous decades.

"May I kiss you good night?"

"Go right ahead," said Naomi, who appeared to contradict herself by turning her head away.

He found her mouth all the same, enjoying the freshness of it, the clean gardenia scent, and feeling the alarming size of her breasts against him.

Instinctively, he lowered one hand, which she slapped away.

"Please, Mr. Kleiner," she said. "A kiss is one thing. But I'll go wild if you touch me on the *toches*."

The harsh Yiddish phrases, the crazy poem, even the romance with a penis expert—the whole package was so unlikely it made his head spin. Yet when he returned to his room, he could think of nothing but Naomi Glickstein. What puzzled him was that his preference in women had always ranged from the heartbreaking gamin—did anyone feel the loss of Audrey Hepburn more than Kleiner?—to the thin, windswept blonde who spoke in the accent of good schools. The very mention of Bryn Mawr was arousing, though he knew little of its academic standards. So how to account for his powerful feelings toward Naomi Glickstein? Had he been deluding himself, waiting all his life for a big-breasted Borscht Belt beauty? Time would tell. Disgracefully, as he stood beneath the shower, he thought of those massive breasts; at the moment he would have sacrificed a small finger, or at least the top joint, for a look at them. (The thought was no doubt engendered by the harsh penal codes of the Middle East.) To the best of his knowledge, he had no particular fixation on breasts. He had always prided himself on a civilized appreciation of the whole package, so to speak. But here too he may have been papering over another deep longing.

As he considered this, he realized that his penis was erect, marking the triumphant arrival of his first hard-on in the Holy Land. This was welcome news, of course, although, on the downside, there was little he could do, other than to wish it well. Forcing his thoughts in another direction, he toweled himself down and slipped into the robe that had so generously been provided by the management.

Waiting for him in the next room was the Arab who had made him uncomfortable the previous night.

"Good evening, Mr. Kleiner," said Mahmoud, fluffing up his bed pillows. "May I run your bath?"

"I just took a shower. And I thought you weren't going to come in without knocking."

"Of course, sir," said Mahmoud, deftly removing a crease from the sheets. "I'll just be another minute. And by the way, have you spoken to your important friends about my brother's wedding?"

"No. I told you I don't have any."

"You'll help me," said Mahmoud, with gentle confidence. "I know you will. You're a kind man and I know you don't want me to suffer. And you look tired, Mr. Kleiner. Let me rub your feet."

"That won't be necessary. Now, if you don't mind, I'd like to get some sleep."

"It will make you feel better," said Mahmoud. "Mark my words.

"Here," he said, dropping to his knees and swiftly reaching into Kleiner's robe. "First I'll make sexy."

Kleiner shoved him away, then punched him and felt the Arab's nose explode. Raising his hands to his face, as if in prayer, Mahmoud brought them away and stared in horror at blood and bone. Then he threw his head back and let out a terrible sound that might have come from the bazaar, the combination of a camel braying and the cry of a neglected baby.

Nnnnnnnnnnnaaaaaaaaaagggggggghhhhhh.

He ran out the door. Kleiner followed, attempting to offer some sort of apology, but the Arab disappeared quickly, the horrible braying sound continuing to echo through the hallway.

Kleiner returned to his room a shaken man. Why had he reacted so violently? It's possible that the Arab had caught a glimpse of his erection. On a compassionate basis, he was merely trying to be of assistance—which may have been everyday stuff in the circles in which he traveled. Possibly, Mahmoud thought *he* was the one who brought about Kleiner's aroused state, an honest mistake, since the Arab had no way of knowing about Naomi Glickstein's contribution.

He was disgusted by his behavior. There had been no justifiable need to smash the young man's face.

He looked at his bloody fist and saw that one knuckle had begun to swell, evidence of a possible broken bone. Sleep was out of the question. After washing off the hand, he put a towel around it and set out to see if he could find the wounded Arab and at least offer him medical attention. There must have been a thousand doctors within shooting distance. Surely one could be induced to make a house call, despite the late hour.

"I'm trying to locate one of your employees," he told the Viennese concierge in the deserted lobby. "A man named Mahmoud."

"I'm sorry, sir. There are no Mahmouds in the hotel."

"But that's impossible. He works in room service."

"See for yourself," said the concierge, producing a roster of employees.

Kleiner scanned the list and saw Abus and Yasins, but as the concierge had attested, no Mahmouds.

"I know he works here," said Kleiner "I just punched him in the face."

"That's hardly proof of employment."

"Maybe he goes by another name."

"If it's Finkelstein, I can help you."

"It wouldn't be Finkelstein," said Kleiner thoughtfully as the concierge closed his book. "Is there a bar that's open at this hour?"

"A bar and grill. But they don't serve Kosher."

"I can live with that," said Kleiner. "I'm wired. I need to unwind."

"The whole country is wired," said the concierge, scribbling on a notepad. "Why should you be different?"

Kleiner found the place easily enough and joined the crowd at the bar, a raffish, hard-drinking group, some of whom openly discussed arms deals and hinted of ties to the IRA. With his bloodshot eyes and bandaged fist, Kleiner felt right at home. To further establish his bona fides, he ordered a double shot of a harsh off-brand whiskey.

Raising his glass untypically, he toasted the bearded and broken-toothed man on the next stool.

"Here's mud in your eye."

Taken aback at first, the man recovered and introduced himself as Moskowitz, an architect who had moved to Jerusalem for the unique pinkish stone and what he called "the clime."

"It seems to have agreed with you. What are you, sixty?" asked Kleiner, charitably shaving a few years from his estimate of the man's age.

"Forty-two," said Moskowitz, who turned away.

The architect was soon joined by a handsome young woman with a strong jaw who wore her blond hair in a crown of ringlets.

When she spoke, it was with a German accent: "You were going to explain your surname."

"I told you," said Moskowitz with exasperation. "It's Hungarian. What do you want from my life?"

Raising a suspicious eyebrow, she said, "That isn't quite what I mean."

She turned her head. Was it Kleiner's imagination or had she whispered "*Judischer*"? Or was it perhaps "*pisher*"?

Kleiner was astonished that an interrogation of this kind could take place in the Great State of Israel. No one was being pulled off to a death camp, but still.

Moskowitz looked at Kleiner.

"Can you believe this! Her father was a U-boat commander and she's worried about my surname."

Once again, Kleiner found himself meddling in someone else's business.

"She's lucky she's not being torn from head to foot. Tell her to get lost."

"I would," said Moskowitz in a whisper. "But there's a chance I can dance in her pants."

"In that case," said Kleiner with a philosophical wave.

When the woman left for the powder room, Kleiner asked the old Jerusalem hand if it was possible for an Arab in a four-star hotel to disappear without a trace.

"Happens all the time."

"What if I wanted to locate such a man?"

"Let him find *you*. If you go looking, they'll rip your dick off."

"Metaphorically speaking, of course."

"I'm an architect. I don't speak in metaphors."

"I see," said Kleiner.

When the woman returned, Kleiner shifted his attention to a table in the rear, where a group of youthful IDF troops, half of them men, half women, sang Israeli war songs. The men were thin and scholarly looking. In the States, they would have been consigned to biology classes. As baseball players, they would be positioned in right field. The women were hopelessly beautiful in their open-collared denim uniforms. They signaled the end of each verse by firing their Galils out the window. On the spot, Kleiner decided to call off his search for Mahmoud and left.

Kleiner awoke the next morning with a fist the size of a grapefruit. After soaking it in warm water, he reviewed his situation. In all innocence, he'd come to Israel to scout a few locations. Already he'd lusted after a Jewish girl's tits and smashed the nose of an Arab in room service. He was just the type of person they needed during the delicate peace negotiations.

Not wanting to get into a long explanation about his fist,

Kleiner told Hilly on the phone that he wanted to nose around on his own for a while.

"Fine," said Hilly, "but if you run into my wife, tell her I spent the night in the hotel with you."

Kleiner didn't think it likely he'd run into the Israeli's wife in a city of millions. Still, and with reluctance, he agreed to be a partner in the deception.

"I appreciate this," said Hilly, "and I owe you one. But be careful or she'll tear off my *schvonce*."

Kleiner winced at what he hoped was only a voguish local expression, although it was becoming apparent that dicks were actually being ripped off in Jerusalem, or at least a few.

Kleiner began his day with a sacred pilgrimage to the Holocaust Memorial at Yad Vashem. Though his only personal loss in the Jews' greatest tragedy was a few distant cousins by marriage, Kleiner himself had suffered a mysterious weight loss as a child in 1941; he had pictorial evidence to prove it. Medicine and injections were of no avail. He'd even been sent to a special upstate facility to fatten him up with milkshakes. But nothing worked; though he was remarkably cheerful, he remained a bag of bones. His parents were distraught; the doctors threw up their hands. Then, just as he was about to go down the tubes, the camps were liberated in '45. On that very day, Kleiner began to gain weight again, becoming a fat guy for a while.

For the most part, Kleiner kept this part of his history to himself. He had only told a few dates at college about it. But in his soul he was convinced that there was a connection between the Nazi horror and the plight of a ridiculously skinny kid in faraway Washington Heights. Not that he felt he was entitled to reparations from the new German Republic.

Such were his thoughts as he looked at the pictures—by now familiar—of people who had actually suffered in the camps.

"What do you think?" he asked a cute girl who had a borough accent.

"Fucking unreal."

Kleiner stood on line to put his name in the visitors' book. When it was his turn, he wrote simply:

> *With Respect,*
> *William Kleiner*

The man behind him read his inscription and called out bitterly, "Is that the best you can do?"

"There was a lot of feeling in it," said Kleiner, who admitted inwardly that he may have gone too far in understatement. At the same time, he didn't appreciate getting rewrite notes at a Holocaust memorial.

He asked the ancient groundskeeper, "How do the Germans react?"

"They don't," said the man as he swept up leaves.

"They're silent?"

"What should they do, make jokes?"

Kleiner returned to the Arab Quarter and redemptively bought a credit-card holder, although not from the vendor who had warned him never to turn his back in Jerusalem. Then he stood on line to enter the Chapel of the Ascension, where Christ was alleged to have risen from the dead—although some argued that he had lifted off a few miles away. A touring group of Greek widows stood in front of Kleiner. Behind him were stocky blond fundamentalists from Chicago.

When it was Kleiner's turn to enter the holy site, he had to crouch down to enter the passageway. It soon became apparent that he had miscalculated the amount of space inside the tomb. Surely money could be raised for an expansion. Authenticity no doubt had won out. Still, the limited space was a problem for Kleiner, who was claustrophobic; he'd once had to be removed unconscious from a submarine outside of St. Croix, where he'd gone to scout a location.

Kleiner took a quick respectful look at the crucifixion site, then tried to back his way out of the small musty cavern. By this time, the fundamentalists had come bouncing in on powerful haunches, blocking the exit. Contorting their bodies, they cried out in tongues, a language the devout Chicagoans seemed to make up as they went along. *N-n-n-n-n——g-g-g—g—ngnghhhhhh—* A guidebook said the angels could translate these sounds into simple English. Kleiner wished them luck. Short of breath, he fell to his knees and tried to crawl through a thicket of powerful blond legs as they pumped away with sincere religious ecstasy. He began to lose consciousness. It occurred to him that if he dropped dead in Christ's tomb, it would be construed—if anyone bothered to construe it—as a cheap bid for immortality by a failed Jew in the movie business. At most, after his death, he would attract a few dozen followers—a mixed bag of renegade Yeshiva students and a few regulars at comic-book conventions.

Finally, he worked his way through one last pair of straining fundamentalist haunches and reached the outside passage. Hyperventilating, he shoved aside a frail nun and collapsed on the marble slab that was used to rinse Christ's wounds. A white light appeared to him; he tasted a sweet sinusoidal liquid that was not unpleasant and blacked out.

When he came to, he found himself being gently rocked back and forth. He thought for a moment he might be riding a camel through the clouds. Looking around to get his bearings, he saw that he was in a harness that was strapped to the powerful shoulders of a man who was parading him through the streets of Jerusalem.

"What's going on?" he asked the man.

The rescuer turned his head slightly. It was Mahmoud.

"I'm taking you to the clinic, Mr. Kleiner. You fell and cracked your head."

Kleiner put his hand to his temple and felt a large gash. How large, he tried not to speculate.

Still, he couldn't resist saying, "Feels like I'll need a stitch or two."

Mahmoud corrected him.

"Nine," said the Arab.

"Don't they have an ambulance?"

He assumed that visitors to the Old City were overcome by religious ecstasy every day of the week and would require medical attention.

"They had to cancel it because of budgetary considerations. Now they depend on Arabs such as myself to assist the stricken. I was filling in—after they threw me out of the hotel—and I was happy to see that I was there when you passed out."

"I can walk," said Kleiner proudly.

"Of course. But why upset yourself. Let someone else help you for a change."

The young Arab's words rang true. Kleiner had trouble accepting favors. But he gave it a try and allowed himself to be rocked into a coma.

When he came to, he was in the waiting room of a clinic, with Mahmoud carefully watching over him. The doctor in attendance was a man of roughly Kleiner's age. He wore a kippah and a prayer shawl and appeared to have rushed right over from the synagogue.

"You're all right," he said, taking Kleiner by the shoulders. "There's nothing wrong with you.

"You *must* believe me," he added, almost pleading at this point.

"What about my head?"

"That's a very big problem," said the doctor. "But basically, you're fine."

The doctor stitched up Kleiner's head and bandaged his fist properly. Then he presented a bill for the head wound. It seemed quite reasonable.

"And my hand?" asked Kleiner.

"I threw that in."

Then the doctor stared at him with moist eyes. "Remember, we're not as young as we used to be."

Kleiner tried to follow the doctor's logic. Was he suggesting that it was all right to split your head open in Christ's tomb when you're a young man, but that it's inadvisable when you get older?

As he considered this, the traumatic experience in the tomb caught up with him. His knees gave way. Mahmoud, who had been playing bingo with another patient, came running over to steady him.

"You're coming home with me," he said firmly, "until you're on your feet."

"What's wrong with the hotel?"

"I'm dead meat there. Besides, it's too gloomy."

"All right," said Kleiner. "But I'm not traveling on your back."

"Of course not," said Mahmoud. "We'll take a limo."

Shortly thereafter, a stretch pulled up to the clinic. Kleiner and Mahmoud shared it with two Jews for Jesus who were under indictment for insisting that Christ was the Messiah.

"Do you really think he is?" asked Kleiner.

"Absolutely," said one of the cultists.

The other tapped an attaché case.

"We have the proof right in here."

The car dropped Kleiner and Mahmoud off in the Old City. The Jews continued on, no doubt to make their point. The result could only mean more trouble for the Jews. But at least they had a purpose in life.

The Arab led the American to a dark apartment on the second floor of a shabby building. The ceilings were low, the lights dim. The rugs that covered the stone floor were on the dark side too.

"This isn't gloomy?" said Kleiner.

"Not when you get used to it."

When Kleiner's eyes had adjusted to the light, he saw that the lamps were antiques, the rugs richly brocaded; handsome tapestries covered the walls. This surprised him. He had assumed that the Arab lived under a rock somewhere.

On the walls, unaccountably, were signed glossy photographs of Bobby Darin and Liza Minnelli. Was it possible Mahmoud's family were intimates of the show-business luminaries?

"They only visited for two minutes," said Mahmoud.

"But still . . ." said Kleiner. He looked around. "Actually, it's quite comfortable."

The Arab responded with pride. "My father is in real estate. He owns practically half the souk."

A stout, middle-aged woman entered the room. She glared at Kleiner, then left.

"That's my mother," said Mahmoud with pride.

"Did I do something to offend?"

"No, no. That's her way of showing that she likes you."

A burly, pipe-smoking man wearing a robe and sandals entered the room. He introduced himself as Farid Salah, the father of Mahmoud.

"Welcome," he said. "My home is at your disposal. I appreciate all you've done for my son."

"Not at all," said Kleiner, who frankly couldn't understand how smashing the boy's nose had contributed to his welfare.

"The flesh heals," said Mr. Salah, with a philosophical puff of his pipe. "But you got him out of room service."

At that point, he clapped his hands and his wife appeared, carrying two bowls of a steaming concoction. After glaring at Kleiner again, but also at her husband, she set the bowls down on a table and left.

Mahmoud confessed he had eaten a pizza earlier in the day and had little appetite. He excused himself and left the two men alone in the room.

"Special hummus," said Mr. Salah. "It's a recipe that's been in the family for generations. Many have begged me to commercialize it, but each time I've refused. Please don't ask me how it's made."

Kleiner was slightly offended. Did the Arab think he had nothing better to do than sit around and grind chickpeas, following some arcane specifications?

"I wouldn't think of it."

"Good. Give it a try."

After tasting the dish, Kleiner saw that its secret was worth guarding. Few dishes were capable of changing his life—but this may have been one of them.

When they had finished their meal, Mr. Salah said, "I wouldn't pay much attention to the wedding."

"But it means so much to him."

"A phase," said Mr. Salah, waving off Kleiner's words. "My youngest son will get married many times."

Then why let him get married now? Kleiner wondered. But he remained silent, concluding that the ways of the Arab world were complex and foreign to his understanding.

"Would you care to watch a videocassette with me?" asked Mr. Salah after they'd had coffee. "It stars the American actor William Hurt, a favorite of mine."

Kleiner admired Hurt as well, but didn't think he could watch one of his slow-paced movies with stitches in his head.

"I'd better get back."

"Then let me give you this," said Mr. Salah.

He reached into a cabinet and took out a quart bottle of what appeared to be the treasured hummus.

"For the hotel," he said, handing it to Kleiner. "Make sure it's heated at an even temperature."

Kleiner thanked the congenial Arab, then entered Mahmoud's room to say goodbye.

The young Arab was resting peacefully on a divan.

"Your father is a wonderful man."

"If one could follow in his footsteps."

"One can."

Kleiner looked around the neatly kept room. There were tropical fish in a tank, a high school diploma, toy dinosaurs on a desk. On a shelf, the complete works of the great Egyptian novelist Naguib Mahfouz. Also, a copy of *Number One with a Bullet*, an exposé of the recording industry. On the walls were pictures of Mahmoud, riding a pony in the desert, blowing out birthday candles, kneeling with a protective arm around a younger man who resembled him and might have been his brother.

Kleiner turned to Mahmoud and looked at him, as if for the first time. His hair was thinning slightly, his eyes were green and clear; the nose that Kleiner had smashed was flattened out now, giving him the look of a Plains Indian. In a rush of emotion, he put his arms around the young Arab, pulled him to his chest, and with tears in his eyes, said:

"I will take you to LeFrak City."

PART TWO

The girl that I marry. New Haven. Traffic court. A justice of the peace. Kleiner's idea. Emma, wildflowers in her hair. Becky clinging to his leg. It was Kleiner's second try at marriage. This time he'd get it right.

A brave promise, indeed, but could Kleiner carry it out? If he showed up at the airport with a controversial Arab, the Israelis would laugh in his face. And obviously, you couldn't just stroll across Israel's borders, which were ringed with hostile states. That included Egypt, which was a little less hostile. A Jew and an Arab would be shot on sight, and that's if they were lucky. Additionally, the Israelis had made it perfectly clear they wanted Mahmoud to stay right where he was, so they could keep an eye on him.

How had Kleiner gotten himself into this situation?

It's true that Mahmoud had carried him on his back to the clinic and no doubt saved his life. Yet that alone did not entirely explain the obligation he felt toward the Arab. It was only when Kleiner had looked at the contents of Mahmoud's room—and saw that he was a boy like any other—that he decided to enter into this strange and seemingly hopeless compact.

Kleiner called for a cab to take him back to the hotel.

"Sit tight," he told Mahmoud, reaching over to give him another hug.

The Arab drew away from him.

"Enough is enough," he said. "And how am I supposed to relax when the wedding is in two days?"

"I need time to think," said Kleiner. "This is new territory for me."

All along, Kleiner had insisted he was without powerful friends, which wasn't quite true. He had one, Louis Blumenthal, an influential fund-raiser and pro-Israel lobbyist who had been known to leap over restaurant tables to confront diners he suspected of harboring negative feelings about the Jewish state. A fiery little rooster of a man, Blumenthal was five feet tall and bald, yet saw himself as Cary Grant and moved like a dancer. Incredibly, he had a long list of romantic conquests, many of them brassiere models. He had a henchman who kept an eye out for hefty candidates. Blumenthal had been made an honorary general in the Israeli Army; on his trips to Jerusalem—he never stayed long—he was immediately flown to the borders for a look at the country's strategic fortifications and to see the dangers it faced.

The two had remained friends since college, mostly because Blumenthal had once seen Kleiner, in a tuxedo, stroll into the Waldorf-Astoria with Clint Eastwood. It was an accident— the two had been forced to share a cab in the rain. There was little communication between Kleiner and the star—a brief exchange about Eastwood's profit participation in *The Good, the Bad and the Ugly*—but Blumenthal was convinced that Kleiner had major connections in the film industry and would be able to work him into it in some capacity.

The trouble with Blumenthal is that he was notorious for demanding huge favors in return for his assistance. For this reason, Kleiner had been careful not to ask him to so much as pass the salt, fearing what it would cost him in the future. But if anyone could reach the levers of power in Israel, it was Louis Blumenthal.

When he arrived at the hotel, Kleiner called Blumenthal and reached him at his flat, which was only a few yards away from the Stage Delicatessen—in case, God forbid, he was caught short for a pastrami sandwich.

"What are you doing in Israel?" asked Blumenthal.

Kleiner heard moaning in the background.

"For Christ's sakes," Blumenthal said, no doubt to one of his brassiere models, "can you at least stop for two minutes?"

"And you can't call him back?" the woman's voice pleaded.

"We can pick it up, Tiffany," he said. "We got another half hour."

"Hef would never have taken the call."

Blumenthal seemed amazed that someone had traveled to the Jewish state without first consulting him.

"Dayan would have flown you over the borders to show you why we can't give up an inch of territory."

"I didn't want to bother you," said Kleiner. "I'm working on a movie."

"So we'll work on it together," said Blumenthal. "What's it about?"

"It's a Jewish *Star Wars*. But I'm only a location scout."

"Bullshit. You can squeeze me in."

Aware that he was making a mistake, Kleiner said vaguely that he'd see what he could do. Then he told Blumenthal he'd met someone in room service at the King David and promised to help him attend a wedding in LeFrak City.

"The Israelis are giving him a hard time and I need your help."

"Why are you bothering me with this shit? And Tiffany, can you leave the *petzel* alone for two minutes? Oh, so now it's a *petzelah*? You're lucky I got you a job. Now, where were we?"

"It means a lot to me," said Kleiner.

"All right," said Blumenthal with a sigh. "What's his name?"

"Mahmoud Salah."

"An Arab?"

Kleiner could see Blumenthal setting aside his huge Macanudo cigar.

"Yes, but he's more than that. If you met him, you'd understand what I mean."

"You're getting crazier by the minute," said Blumenthal. A right-wing lunatic when it came to Israel, he also had a maverick side. "I'll make a few phone calls."

"Thank you, Louis," said Kleiner. "And how are you getting along?"

He was pleased with himself for asking the question, having coached himself to inquire about other people's fortunes even when he wasn't that interested.

"I'm a little short," said Blumenthal. "A lousy ten grand would set me straight."

"I see," said Kleiner, who was sorry he had asked.

There was a pause that seemed to last two hours. He thought about his credit-card debt, and the few dollars he had in the bank for an emergency. Did the Arab's situation fall into that category? Mercifully, Blumenthal broke the silence and said he'd get back to Kleiner.

With the influential lobbyist working on his behalf, Kleiner allowed himself to relax and prepare for bed. In the bathroom, he lifted the bandage on his head to check his wound, then slapped it back in horror. Though the doctor's work was elegant and meticulous, the wound had been stitched in such a way that it resembled a fragment of the Dead Sea scrolls. In the future, whenever Kleiner entered a restaurant or ordered a drink at a bar, his head would boldly announce his heritage—as if his face wasn't enough.

Kleiner slept fitfully. He had a troubling dream in which all the books in his local library, including the technical manuals, were written by Joyce Carol Oates. Kleiner prided himself on being able to unlock the secrets of his dreams. But try as he might he was unable to establish a connection between the bookish nightmare and his plan to help an Arab make a getaway to Queens. (An escape from the thunderous output of Oates? Absurd, since he admired much of her work, particularly the short stories.)

Responsibly, Kleiner scouted a few locations the next day—some Stations of the Cross that he had overlooked—and the Knesset, where Hilly arranged for him to sit in Shamir's old seat.

"How does it feel?" asked Hilly as Kleiner made himself comfortable and pretended he was introducing a housing bill.

"Like a million dollars."

Later in the day, the two men repaired to the hell-for-leather little bar on Netanyu Street.

"Some important business has come up," he told Hilly. "I have to cut my trip short."

Hilly said he was sorry to hear that. The two men embraced.

"Goodbye, old friend," said Hilly, as if they were wartime comrades.

As it happened, Kleiner had served as a supply sergeant in Korea—so he didn't feel like a total fraud.

"We've come so far and been through so much," the Israeli continued.

Here too Kleiner disagreed, but saw no reason to contradict his emotional friend.

"Next time you come to Israel, I hope you rent an apartment and become a real Jew for a change.

"If not," he added ruefully, "maybe you can find something for me in New York. I've been thinking of a switch to hotel management."

The two men parted. Kleiner, though he barely knew the Israeli, was strangely moved by the separation. It seemed to him that every two seconds the fates arranged for him to say goodbye to someone. All of it, of course, leading up to the final send-off. Was it worth it to say hello?

At the hotel, he checked his messages to see if there was any word from Blumenthal. When such was not the case, he phoned the lobbyist, who said he was sorry but that he couldn't do anything after all.

"I tried Sharon, but Arik is out of the country. Everyone else is on vacation . . . Bibi, the young kid Begin, you name it."

"What do you recommend?"

"Forget it," said Blumenthal. "It was a cockamamie idea to begin with. I checked on your Arab, and he is not taken seriously."

"But that's just it. *I* take him seriously."

"You're wasting your time. And next time you go to Israel, maybe you'll check with me in advance."

Kleiner was surprised and disappointed when he hung up the phone. For all of the boasting about his prestige in Israel, Blumenthal had come up empty in the crunch. Either that or he hadn't even tried to help. Maybe Blumenthal had expected Kleiner to wire him the ten thousand. It would have had to come out of a shaky pension fund, his only assets.

Whatever the case, Kleiner saw that he would have to go

it alone. Normally, he was a man who needed help to tie a shoelace. But when pressed to the wall, he felt he was as good as anyone. Unaided, he'd once found his way out of a hopeless traffic jam in the nation's capital. When it came to mechanics, he thought of himself as being all thumbs. Yet trapped in a summer cottage in rural Maine, he'd installed a VCR.

Buoyed by these recollections, Kleiner opened his atlas and studied Israel's precarious position on the map—as well as his own. How could he and Mahmoud slip out of the country without attracting undue attention?

Immediately he ruled out Syria as an escape route. It was his feeling that even if the Golan Heights were handed over on a platter, Damascus would remain unfriendly to the Jews. He knew this from personal experience, having had to confront a pair of Syrians in a casino in Cap d'Antibes when they'd prayed for him to lose at blackjack.

"*Basse, basse,*" they'd muttered, confident he didn't understand French, which to a certain extent he did.

Jordan, too, was an unattractive option. He pictured Mahmoud and himself being kept under guard in a once-grand but now-shabby hotel, with only basic amenities while the Hashemites conducted endless arguments over their fate.

That left Egypt—aloof, enigmatic, not friendly, not entirely hostile. He felt that after a day or two of Sphinx-like considerations, the Egyptians, drawing on ancient diplomatic skills, would send them on their way, prepared to stand up to Israel which needed at least one quiet neighbor on its borders—and a potentially strong trading partner.

Kleiner misplaced a sweater and thought he'd check Emma's closet. A shower of pills and empty vodka bottles came raining down on his head. He packed a suitcase and was gone.

. . .

Kleiner looked at the southernmost tip of Israel and saw that it was only a hop, skip, and a jump from the Sinai. The thought ran through his head that Mike Kleiner, a favorite uncle who had gone in after Pancho Villa in the Mexican War—was an Anwar Sadat lookalike.

With a dramatic flourish, he circled the city of Eilat.

Having made his decision, Kleiner called Mahmoud and told him to prepare to leave Jerusalem at dawn, taking along as little as possible.

"Ideally, just what you can carry on your person."

"That's impossible," said the young Arab. "It's a formal wedding. I have to bring a tuxedo, spats—"

"Can we forget spats?" said Kleiner with irritation. "This is not about spats. And you can rent a tux in New York."

"I wear a forty-two long. With all respect, Mr. Kleiner, I'll need at least two suitcases."

"That's out of the question."

"Then why don't we forget it? I'll send my brother a present and we can save ourselves a lot of trouble."

"Now, look," said Kleiner in a fury. "You're *going* to that wedding. I didn't come this far to call the whole thing off."

"All right, Mr. Kleiner," said Mahmoud with a sigh. "But remember, this was your idea."

Kleiner hung up, amazed at his own behavior. The Arab had given him an out. Why hadn't he taken it and run like a thief? For one thing, he felt that Mahmoud's change of heart was insincere. He knew how passionately the young Arab wanted to attend his brother's wedding. More to the point was a flaw in Kleiner's basic nature—an inability to change direction, which had been costly to him in sports, dancing, and lovemaking, to name just a few of the troubled areas. Once embarked on a course of action, he remained committed to it, even when it was patiently explained to him that he was making a fool of himself. Some called this insecurity. Most didn't bother to call it anything.

With little time to be lustful, Kleiner nonetheless called Naomi Glickstein to say goodbye.

"I'm so glad you called," she said. "Can you come by my room? I have something to show you."

Kleiner abandoned his plan to get a good night's sleep in preparation for the dangerous journey.

"I'll be right over."

As he entered her room, Kleiner noted with some disappointment that Naomi was wearing another of her tailored career-woman outfits. He wondered if she slept in one.

"Look," she said, pointing to a videocassette on the cocktail table. "I ordered it up from the concierge."

Kleiner glanced at the label and saw that it was his first and possibly only successful movie, at least in terms of the critical reception.

"You're a classic, Kleiner," she said, taking both of his hands. "I had no idea."

"What did you think of it?"

"I haven't watched it yet, but I recall Sol saying it was excellent, especially the first half."

"The second half had merit too."

"I'm going to put it on as soon as I do my nails. But why are you leaving so fast? And what happened to your head?"

"I cracked it in the Chapel of the Ascension."

"No wonder you're leaving," she said.

"That's not it," said Kleiner.

Though he'd vowed not to tell a soul about his plan, he proceeded to describe it in immaculate detail.

"And this is what you want to do?" said Naomi.

"I have to."

"Then do it," she said with fervor, putting her arms around him. "Or you'll never be able to live with yourself. And take me with you."

Kleiner tried to imagine what it would be like to show up in Cairo not only with Mahmoud but also the Yiddish-speaking Naomi in a string bikini.

"It wouldn't work out."

She pressed her damp and fragrant body against him. "Then what can I do to help?"

Kleiner hesitated, then took a chance. "Can I see them?"

"What's that?" asked Naomi.

Then, after a beat, she understood.

"Oh, sure," she said, removing her suit jacket. She unbuttoned her blouse to unhook a fortresslike foundation garment. The effect was tremendously erotic, like watching a CEO undress at a board meeting.

It was impossible for Kleiner to be casual when he saw her enormous breasts. With as much reverence as passion, he kissed each one.

Patiently, she corrected his style.

"I can see you've never dealt with a bubbies girl."

Then, sweeping her hands up through her hair, she flicked on some Tito Puente music and gave her breasts a little shake.

Taking this as a cue, Kleiner pulled her to him, kissed her deeply, and plunged his hand into her surprisingly sensible panties.

"Please," she said, stopping him again. "Not tonight. It's too close to Sol. Not the kugel.

"But here are my numbers in New York," she said, scribbling on a notepad. "The second one is a service and they're a little slow to pick up."

"I'll keep ringing," said Kleiner, folding the slip of paper and putting it in his new credit-card holder. Then he returned to his room, aware that he'd been badly thrown off stride by the last Yiddish expression. He'd stayed with her on *plotz* and *toches* and *meshugge*, but felt she had stepped over the line with kugel as a pet name for her vagina.

Still, Naomi had shown remarkable faith in him, never once questioning his plan to spirit Mahmoud out of Israel so he could show up at a wedding in LeFrak City. He found this abiding faith attractive, although no doubt she'd encouraged Sol to follow *his* star as well—which in the case of the famed urologist meant consulting on additional penises. Her great body notwithstanding, Kleiner admired her blind loyalty. He decided he might just give her a call if he ever made it safely back to Manhattan.

To get a jump on the next day, Kleiner packed his possessions in cartons and labeled them for shipment back to New York. He left out only the bare essentials—a toothbrush, his great form-fitting Speedo swimsuit, and a small survival tool that enabled the user to open bottles, cut through barbed wire, and file his nails.

Then he went to bed, the enormity of what he was attempting to do closing in on him. Over decades, the country of Israel had been constructed with the blood and money of a multitude of Jews. Kleiner himself had sent them a few dollars. Yet what was his major contribution to the Jewish state? Sneaking an Arab out of the country to attend a wedding, when a simple present would have sufficed. What kind of Jew did that make him? And a Jew he'd remain until his dying day. Unless, of course, hostility to his people ended, in which case he would have to think over his options.

Then there were the dangers. If he was caught, he'd been alerted to what would happen to his precious cock. And even if he made it, there was a chance that certain religious rightist groups would put out a contract on him. This would place Kleiner in that most unenviable of positions—a Jew sought 'round the world by other Jews.

Kleiner's last thoughts before he nodded off were of his friend and psychiatrist, a mortality expert, who had dropped dead suddenly before he'd given Kleiner any tips on dying.

Kleiner checked out the next morning and raced over to Mahmoud's apartment, there to be greeted by Mr. Salah in a black and white kaffiyeh of the kind worn by Yasser Arafat at press conferences. In the background, Kleiner could see Mrs. Salah rolling around on the carpet, beating her breast and crying out her son's name.

"Forgive my wife," said Mr. Salah. "She's concerned about the soaring crime statistics in the territories."

"Queens is a territory?"

"*Inshallah,*" said the elderly Arab.

He went into the bedroom to rouse his sleeping son, then joined Kleiner in the living room.

"I'll concede that my son can be testy," he said as he poured a cup of coffee for Kleiner. "But if he acts up, don't smash him in the face again."

Kleiner assured him there was little likelihood he would do so.

"I hope not," said Mr. Salah, sternly. "Once was enough."

Freshly shaved, smelling of Old Spice, Mahmoud appeared and greeted Kleiner warmly. Then, while Kleiner waited with impatience, he ate a huge breakfast that his mother had prepared for him.

When he'd finished the last of the eggs and beans, his father pressed a twenty-dollar bill in his hand and warned him to take the proper precautions if he should get involved with the women of Queens.

Mahmoud bid his parents farewell. The two men set out on their precarious journey.

They made it to the street outside the walled city. Kleiner was thrilled they had gotten that far without being thrown into prison. Furtively, Kleiner looked for a cab while at the same time preparing a story in case they got stopped.

I'm just taking a three-hundred-mile drive to the border with an Arab I met in room service.

Obviously, there were holes in the account, but it was the best he could do at the moment.

If Mahmoud felt any apprehension, he didn't show it. Nonchalantly, he stood beside Kleiner, sucking on a toothpick, one hip thrown out in the style of a male hustler.

When a cab finally stopped for them, the two men jumped in. Kleiner was amazed to see that the driver was the stocky Pole who had first taken him to the King David. The man recognized Kleiner immediately and embraced him with a bear hug.

"You have no idea what you did for me," said the driver.

"After we met, I threw my children out on the street and I felt a hundred pounds lighter."

"I'm glad I could help," said Kleiner.

"I can't thank you enough. To think I was still feeding them when they were forty."

"Is he going to carry on this way for the whole trip?" said the Arab. "Because frankly, Mr. Kleiner, I had a troubled sleep last night."

"Let him show his gratitude."

"Thank you," said the driver with a sharp look at Mahmoud. "And where may I take you?"

"Eilat," said Kleiner.

"That's a long trip," said the driver. "And I'll probably have to come back empty. I wish I didn't have to charge you, but even without the kids, I still feel squeezed."

"Put it out of your mind," said Kleiner.

The driver sped off. Before long, the rocky motion of the cab had lulled both passengers to sleep. Sometime later, they came to a roadblock and were flagged over to the side by a uniformed soldier who asked to see their identification. Kleiner handed him his passport, Mahmoud his ID. As the soldier reviewed the documents, Kleiner considered making a full confession and having his records faxed over from the States. They would show that he hadn't broken a law since the fifth grade, when he had accidentally stolen a pencil sharpener.

Apparently satisfied, the soldier handed back the papers, then nodded toward Mahmoud.

"Why do you travel with *schmutz*?"

Kleiner answered with uncharacteristic bravery, still clinging to the belief that a Jew would never harm him.

"If he's *schmutz*, then I'm an Arab."

In this case, Kleiner was right; with a snort, the soldier directed them to join a mixed group of travelers behind a barricade.

"You didn't have to do that for me," said Mahmoud.

"Who said he did it for you?" said the driver with surprising insight.

Behind the barricade, a bejeweled young woman from California paced up and down nervously, stopping only to tell an uncomprehending group of Druse that she had once dated Joe Namath.

Kleiner also recognized yet another woman from the lobby of the King David. She complained to her husband that a soldier had been rude to her.

"Should I make a stink?"

"That's up to you, darling," her husband said neutrally.

A bomb-squad truck rolled up. Two men in tank suits jumped out and fell to the ground as if they were being fired upon. Their bellies hugging the dirt, they began to play out a long black coil, which they manipulated to examine a suspicious-looking brown bag that had been left on a bench. After twenty minutes, one of them declared that it was only a harmless ham and cheese sandwich.

"You can all be on your way," he told the detainees.

"And for this you tie up the whole city?" complained the driver.

"You can't be too careful," said the man. "Yesterday we had a tuna on rye go up outside the Knesset."

The three men piled back into the cab and continued their journey. When they reached the port of Eilat, Kleiner paid the driver, who thanked him once again for his help in kicking out his children.

"I can't give you money," said the grateful driver, "but I do horoscopes on the side. Next time you're in Jerusalem, I promise you a reading on the house."

Kleiner expressed his appreciation. Then the driver sped off. The two remaining men walked down to the shore just in time to board an excursion boat as it pulled into the Gulf of Aqaba.

Kleiner paid the fare. On the top deck, the two men joined a group of tourists, who were listening to a guide as he pointed out rare specimens of marine life.

"There before you," he said, gesturing toward a reef, "is a beautiful cluster of closed beadlet anemones."

"He's wrong," Mahmoud said to Kleiner. "Those are open periwinkles."

"Don't correct him," said Kleiner.

For obvious reasons he was anxious to keep a low profile.

"But they'll go away thinking they saw something they didn't see. I think it's disgraceful."

"Who cares?" said Kleiner. "And incidentally, where did you learn this?"

"At Jew school," said Mahmoud.

"*Jewish* school," Kleiner corrected him angrily.

"Whatever."

The guide drew the attention of the group to a thicket of limestone date mussels.

"Only in Israel will you find them," he said with pride.

"He's doing it again," said Mahmoud bitterly. Then he hollered out: "What about St. Bart's?"

"I know about St. Bart's," said the guide with condescension. "And believe me, everybody, when I tell you that the limestone date mussels of St. Bart's are not authentic."

Before Mahmoud could respond, Kleiner yanked at his shirt and the two men slipped below to the abandoned lower deck. Far off in the distance, Kleiner saw what he perceived to be the Egyptian coastline. The vast expanse of sea would have intimidated a normal person, but Kleiner, though his style in the water was laughable, had endurance on his side. He felt that he could swim forever.

The two men stripped down to their swimsuits, Kleiner to his beloved form-fitting Speedo, Mahmoud to an attention-getting leopard-skin bikini that was much too small for him.

Kleiner looked at him with distaste.

"Is that the only suit you have?"

Mahmoud tugged at the garment. He seemed hurt by the question.

"What's wrong with it?"

"Never mind."

Kleiner checked the waterproof waistband that held his valuables, then prepared to slip over the side. Holding on to the railing, he heard grunting sounds and looked back to see Mahmoud doing elaborate splits, his ass exploding out in all directions.

"What are you doing now?" asked Kleiner.

"Stretching my hammies."

Kleiner winced at the phrase—he'd once broken up a romance with a woman who said "veggies" once too often. "Lambies" for lamb chops had been the final straw.

"Hurry up about it," said Kleiner.

Taking his time, Mahmoud did a few more. The two men then dropped quietly into the water.

Pacing himself, Kleiner began his awkward but powerful crawl, while Mahmoud cut through the choppy waters with a crisp and professional breaststroke.

"Where did you learn that?" asked Kleiner, struggling to keep up.

"At Jew camp."

"Jewish camp," said Kleiner, more than annoyed and correcting him again.

"Mr. Kleiner," said Mahmoud, treading water. "I went to camp with Jews. What do you want from my life?"

The two men proceeded for a hundred yards or so; then, suddenly, Mahmoud began to thrash about and to gasp for air.

"I've got a cramp, Mr. Kleiner," said the struggling Arab. "It's probably related to a tendonitis condition in my knee."

"I don't care what it's related to," said Kleiner.

He swam toward the Arab, desperately trying to remember the cross-chest carry he'd learned years back as a junior lifesaver at summer camp in the Berkshires.

"Stay calm," he said, as much to himself as to Mahmoud.

Taking hold of the panicky Arab, he began to inch his way forward. A patrol boat bore down upon them. An officer shouted out a command.

"*Aztor.*"

"Gladly," said Kleiner.

He considered diving below and drowning, but was afraid of drinking all the water such an action would require. Also, he still held out hope of getting a choice directing assignment on the coast.

The two men allowed themselves to be dragged on board by the naval officer, a handsome man with the classic profile of a matinee idol. Kleiner was convinced that at minimum, he could get him work on a television series, although it was far from clear that the Israeli would leave the security of the coast guard for acting roles.

Also on deck was a stout and much less attractive man who wore tennis shoes, sucked on a toothpick, and sleepily leafed through an old swimsuit issue of *Sports Illustrated.*

Kleiner, of course, feared him more than the other. He looked around in vain for a towel.

"What's the story?" asked the handsome officer.

"Very simple," said Kleiner. "I'm in the movie business and I was scouting locations for a movie. What they have in mind is a Jewish *Star Wars*. I can show you my Director's Guild ID if you like."

The officer shook his head. It wasn't necessary.

The second man looked up from his magazine. "And the shit bag?"

In response, Mahmoud began to tremble. Then, in a clear, pure, melodious voice, he broke into a chorus of "Hatikvah."

"Where did he learn that?" asked the handsome officer.

"In Jew camp," said Kleiner.

"*Jewish* camp," said the magazine reader.

With lightning speed, he threw a black hood over the Arab's head. This effectively drowned him out, although Mahmoud did try valiantly to hum a few extra bars.

"Put one on me," said Kleiner, in his new defiant mode.

"We ran out of them," said the man in the sneakers. "But there may be a few on shore."

Back on land, the two men were marched past gawking tourists and taken to a poorly decorated compound, where they were placed in a bare cell. Humanistically, they were supplied with beach towels and each given a bowl of kasha varnishkes.

Kleiner had never been in a cell before. Secretly, he'd longed to try one for a single night, to see how he could handle confinement. Nonetheless, he scolded the Arab for getting them into a mess.

"I don't understand your concern," said Mahmoud. "It's just a routine check."

"At least take off the hood."

"Why? I'm getting used to it."

After a two-hour wait, which was obviously designed to weaken their resolve, a middle-aged man in shirtsleeves entered the cell and sat on the one chair. He was Western in style. Kleiner thought he recognized him as someone who was called upon to do sound bites for CNN during flare-ups in the Middle East.

"All right," the man said. "What's this all about?"

"I demand to speak to my consulate," said Kleiner, who had no idea if the fledgling administration would lift a finger on his behalf.

"Me too," said Mahmoud.

"You don't have one," said the interrogator sharply. "Let's begin again," he continued, directing his question to Kleiner. "Why were you swimming to Egypt with an Arab?"

Before Kleiner could respond, the man with the tennis shoes came running in with a fax transmission.

"He doesn't have to answer that," he said to his superior. "They're friends of Louis Blumenthal and as such are guests of the state."

"My apologies," said the shirt-sleeved official. "There seems to be some mistake. Did you get enough kasha varnishkes?"

"Plenty," said Mahmoud. "But I wouldn't mind a Diet Pepsi."

"We only have Coke," said the magazine reader.

"If I have to . . ." said Mahmoud, making a face.

Kleiner was thrilled that he hadn't been tortured; he knew full well that if they had touched so much as a single toenail, he would have blurted out everything he knew—though it didn't amount to much. His debt to Blumenthal, of course, was enormous, although fortunately, there would be plenty of time to squirm out of it.

Both men were given makeshift clothing.

"Do we get to keep this?" asked Mahmoud, who liked the way the pants fit.

"If you insist," said the man in the sneakers. "But we'd prefer to have it back."

The official with the CNN style asked Kleiner and even Mahmoud if they would like to take in the world-famed Israeli Philharmonic Orchestra.

"And I can arrange a visit to a kibbutz in Galilee, if you so desire."

Kleiner thanked the official but declined, pleading urgent business in Queens.

"Perhaps I can tempt you with a dinner of pupiks at Fink's in Old Jerusalem. I took Paul Newman there and he fainted with joy from the taste."

"Maybe the next time around," said Kleiner.

"By then, there might not *be* an Israel," said the official in a sudden attack of melancholy.

"How can you say such a thing?"

"You never know."

The official's words were disturbing. Was he suggesting that Kleiner stay behind and fight to the last Jew to defend a country he hadn't actually visited yet?

Whatever the case, Kleiner decided to stick to the plan of taking Mahmoud to LeFrak City, basically because it had a nice shape to it.

A government car was brought around for Mahmoud so he could return to the Arab Quarter and pick up his luggage.

Kleiner himself was taken directly to Ben Gurion Airport by the handsome naval officer.

"Are there acting opportunities in L.A.?" the man asked as they sped along the highway.

"Yes," said Kleiner, "but it's important to go there with a job offer and not start from ground zero."

The officer clutched Kleiner's arm. "Do you think I'm right for network television?"

"It's hard to tell—in this situation. But you look great."

"I'll send you my glossies."

"Please," said Kleiner, scribbling down his address.

At the airport, the naval officer saw to it that Kleiner was seated comfortably in the VIP lounge. Before taking his leave, he handed Kleiner a fresh slice of halvah and a stack of *Vanity Fair*—from its heyday under Tina Brown.

Several hours later, Mahmoud returned with his suitcase and was waved through security. It was Kleiner who was pulled aside and subjected to yet another round of irritating questions. This time they wanted to know the names of everyone he'd spoken to in Israel and why he'd spent so much time with a certain Naomi Glickstein.

"She's a nice person," said Kleiner.

He saw no reason to bare his soul and admit it was because she had big tits and spoke Yiddish.

Finally, he was released and joined Mahmoud on the tarmac.

"I can't believe this," said Kleiner. "They let *you* through and break my balls."

"It pays to have influence," said Mahmoud with a chuckle.

Kleiner noted it was the first joke attempted by the Arab since their initial meeting.

Mahmoud put an arm around Kleiner's shoulders and began to lead him toward the aircraft as if he were an invalid.

"That won't be necessary," said Kleiner, pulling away.

"As you wish," said Mahmoud. "And Dad sends his best."

Aboard the plane, both men took seats in Business Class

and began a silent battle for the single armrest that separated them. Kleiner finally took a higher position, conceding the preferred spot to the Arab. Though hardliners would disagree, perhaps this conciliatory attitude—about an armrest—is what was missing in the quest for peace in the Middle East. Kleiner dismissed the thought. Diplomacy was clearly not his strong suit. He may not have had a strong suit.

Kleiner focused his attention on the handsome redheaded stewardess who had been assigned to them. Mahmoud noticed her as well, and the two men began yet another undeclared struggle—this one for her attention. All thoughts of Middle Eastern peace went out the window. How many times had Kleiner heard it said about himself that he was a fine fellow—except when it came to the pursuit of women? Kleiner discreetly made mention of his directorial credits while the Arab entertained her with stories of Gustav Mahler's early fumbling efforts as a composer.

As they headed over the Atlantic, the stewardess excused herself and slipped behind a closed curtain, joining a passenger who had announced, early in the flight, that he was Harrison Ford's dentist.

"She's very attractive," said Kleiner graciously.

"Really?" said Mahmoud. "I didn't think so."

Much thrashing seemed to go on behind the curtain. With some irritation, Kleiner broke off a piece of halvah to calm his nerves. As he raised it to his mouth, a small creature with a long nose popped out of Mahmoud's shirt and snatched it from his fingers, then ducked back in.

"What was that?" asked Kleiner.

"My dog," said Mahmoud. "I couldn't bear to leave him home."

"Why wasn't I told about him?"

"I didn't want to rock the boat."

"Just keep him out of sight," said Kleiner.

He had nothing against dogs but suspected the creature might not actually be one.

"All right," said Mahmoud, "but Yasser needs at least one exercise walk around the cabin."

He paused for a moment.

"And I hope he doesn't die . . . like his brother. For months they couldn't console me."

"He won't die," said Kleiner, who, of course, couldn't guarantee this prognosis.

He turned his back on the infuriating Arab and began to read a series of Russian plays. They were lugubrious in nature, which made for slow going. By the time he'd gotten through *Ivanov*—and the hero had shot himself—the plane was circling JFK.

Kleiner looked out and was impressed as always by the thunder and brightness of the metropolis below.

"Something, isn't it?" he said.

"Yes," said Mahmoud. "But what about Dayton?"

"What about it?" said Kleiner. "You're looking at the greatest city on Earth. How can you ask about Dayton?"

"I can't help it," said Mahmoud. "As a boy I would lie out on the desert and dream of Dayton's wonders."

At this point, Kleiner was ready to drop Mahmoud off at the airport and say goodbye to him forever. But as the plane touched down, the boy turned to him with a look of tears and innocence.

"What you did for me was wonderful, Mr. Kleiner. Someday I too hope to have power and influence in my community, as you have in yours."

"I'm sure you will," said Kleiner.

"Maybe I'll be able to smuggle a Jew out of a place he doesn't want to be."

"You never know."

Though his plan had been to part company with the Arab the second they hit the ground, Kleiner now reversed himself and insisted that Mahmoud stay with him until the wedding.

"That's not necessary," said Mahmoud. "I'll get a room in a filthy tenement."

"Out of the question," said Kleiner. "You're coming home with me."

There was, of course, a measure of guilt in his behavior. To turn an unworldly Arab loose in hell-for-leather Manhattan was borderline irresponsible. And they had come so far. Then, too, Kleiner had spent a lifetime making decisions that were contrary to his best interests.

The two found a cab easily enough and were soon cruising along Northern Boulevard, past fresh new clubs that Kleiner hadn't seen before.

"Titty bars," said Mahmoud, his eyes wide with delight. "Can we stop and go into one?"

"It's late and I'm tired."

"Oh, please, Mr. Kleiner. It will serve as my bachelor party."

"That's for the groom," said Kleiner.

"My brother is not that sort," said Mahmoud sternly.

Kleiner, who in truth didn't have that much to rush home for—and was curious about the new clubs—agreed to make a brief stop.

The one they chose was a huge and drafty place where men from all nations flung money at women who danced on platforms, wearing only boots. When the guest star was announced, Mahmoud, who appeared to know something about her, could not believe his good fortune.

"Melinda Bunns," he said, his eyes shining. "Wait till I tell my friends back home. Do you know how many times I've jerked off over her?"

"I can't imagine," said Kleiner.

The star, a heavy-chested blonde with disproportionately thin legs, danced to a Michael Jackson recording, then twirled erotically on overhead ropes. When her act was concluded, she received enthusiastic applause and climbed down from the ropes to mingle with the patrons.

Mahmoud stepped forward to introduce himself.

"This is a great privilege," he said. "I'm a great admirer of your hooters."

"Why, thank you, sir," said the star. "Where are you boys from?"

"I'm local," said Kleiner.

"And I'm from Israel," said Mahmoud.

"Oh yes, I've heard of it. I understand it's lots of fun."

"We have troubles, too," said Mahmoud gloomily.

"Don't we all," said Melinda, offering one of her breasts for a kiss. "Maybe one of these babies will cheer you up."

Kleiner politely declined, Mahmoud turned away shyly— and only Yasser took her up on the complimentary offer, emerging from the Arab's shirt for a few licks.

"Why, that's the sweetest thing," said Melinda Bunns, patting the mongrel's nose. "Would you believe I've never worked with a dog?"

As they stood in the lobby of Kleiner's building waiting for the elevator, Mahmoud scanned the tenant directory.

"Why isn't your name listed?" he asked Kleiner.

This was a touchy subject. Kleiner explained that he sublet the apartment from Ralph Himmel, his producer, paying only a modest fee for the handsome duplex, a fraction of its worth. But since the arrangement was illegal, he had to live in the building in stealth, slipping in and out with as little fanfare as possible. Also, the producer reserved the right to use the flat as an emergency set for his films. On such occasions, crews would arrive unannounced to gather up Kleiner's furniture, stacking it up in the hallway to make room for their sound and lighting equipment. At the end of the shoot, they would bring back the furniture. In truth, they were conscientious about putting his possessions back in the proper place, right down to the last ashtray.

Still, the loss of privacy was a tremendous price to pay for Kleiner. Admittedly, he lived in luxury—but with a tight stomach. The second he relaxed, the furniture went out the door.

When Mahmoud heard of the arrangement, his eyes narrowed.

"You shouldn't have to live this way," said the Arab, baring his teeth. "I know how to deal with such people. Where can I find this person? Where does he live? I'll go after him with a bat."

"That's a little extreme," said Kleiner, who shared his sentiments entirely. "There's no reason to be so upset. It's a wonderful apartment."

They were joined in the elevator by Kleiner's next-door neighbor, a plump, hairless man in his seventies who carried a pet monkey in his arms. Attached to the UN, he claimed to be a South American. But his carriage was stiff and he spoke with a vaguely middle-European accent, causing Kleiner to suspect him of being an ex-Nazi who had slipped through the net.

"Are you coming to the tenants' meeting?" he asked, a sadistic question, since he was aware that Kleiner lived in the building under a cloud.

Kleiner averted his eyes. "If I have time."

"I understand there's some question as to your legality here. Still, try to be there," said the UN man, petting the monkey and continuing the torture. "I'm sure everyone would love to see you."

The man was saturated with cologne. By the time they reached the top floor, Kleiner was gasping for air, convinced it would take him a week to rid himself of the cloying fragrance.

"Can you believe that cologne?" said Kleiner as he and the Arab approached the apartment.

"Oh, I don't know," said Mahmoud, sniffing at his shirt-sleeves. "I think it's nice."

Though it wasn't his and never would be, Kleiner took pride in the spacious duplex. He gave Mahmoud a quick tour before settling him in the guest bedroom.

Mirrored from floor to ceiling, it had black and silver furnishings, a holdover from Himmel's S&M fling in the '70s.

"Thank you, Mr. Kleiner," said Mahmoud after a quick look around. "I've never had a real boy's room before."

"Now you have," said Kleiner, who was touched by the young man's gratitude.

Exhausted from the long journey, Mahmoud stretched out on the bed. Before long he was fast asleep, with Yasser curled up at his feet. Kleiner covered him with his best blanket and was tempted to kiss his forehead. He held back for fear that the gesture would be misinterpreted. Still, as he looked at the peaceful young Arab and his dog, he felt that in some odd way, for the first time in years, he presided over a household.

Wearily, he went upstairs to his own bedroom, which had walls of white brick and was encased in a glass capsule. On a clear night, he could see a shower of stars. Lying back on the huge bed he had been forced to buy from Himmel, he looked out on the terrace and saw his neighbor's monkey swing by, as if in welcome, to piss on his one bush. Through the walls of the other adjoining apartment, he could hear the hacking cough of a top cardiologist. And on the floor below, Mahmoud cried out in his sleep for the souk, the dog accompanying him with its own thin howl.

With a surprising degree of comfort, Kleiner closed his eyes and was asleep in an instant.

The next morning, Kleiner found Mahmoud sitting cross-legged on the living-room floor, poring over a faded album of pictures he had found in a sealed carton.

"Who gave you permission to do that?" Kleiner asked angrily.

"You have a lovely family," said Mahmoud. "Why be ashamed of them?"

Though the Arab had no business going through his private papers—and the comment was beside the point—Mahmoud had struck a nerve. To a degree, Kleiner *was* ashamed of his parents; they were short in stature. In the photographs, they wore cheap and dated clothing. With a look she took to be seductive, his mother flashed broken gypsy teeth while his father gave off the dull look of failure—at least in business.

"This is my favorite," said Mahmoud, holding up a picture of Kleiner and his father at the base of the Statue of Liberty.

He had always thought of his father as a cold and indifferent man. Yet in the picture, the older man had his arm draped protectively around young Kleiner's shoulders. The picture was taken at a time when Kleiner was no more than a bag of bones, a sympathetic reaction to the horrors of Dachau. It showed clearly that his father loved him after all, even though it had taken an Arab from far-off Jerusalem to point it out.

He thought of his mother's final words: "Make sure to have fun. I certainly did."

It was an excellent legacy that Kleiner had failed to carry out, although he planned to start momentarily.

"I'll take this one," he said, pocketing a picture of his parents together at a wedding. He was determined to have it put in an expensive frame and to take it with him on trips—to make up for the lost years.

"Put the rest away."

Since there was no food in the apartment, the two men had breakfast at a tiny diner on noisy First Avenue. Though Mahmoud insisted he wasn't hungry, he ate his way through half the menu.

"These are the greatest eggs on Earth," said the Arab, who, Kleiner noted, was prone to exaggeration. "I don't know how they do it."

"They're brought in each morning by Palestinians, fresh from New Jersey."

"I should have known."

In the busy street, Mahmoud asked Kleiner for directions to F.A.O. Schwarz so he could buy his brother a present. The fabled toy emporium seemed an unlikely place to find a wedding gift, but Kleiner showed him how to get there anyway. Then he returned to the apartment to sort out his location shots, so that he could FedEx them to Himmel on the coast.

As he sat down at his desk, he noticed a manila envelope propped up against his old-fashioned Remington typewriter—with a note attached.

Dear Mr. Kleiner,
I'd appreciate it if you'd glance at the enclosed—if
you have a moment.

Faithfully, Mahmoud

Kleiner looked inside the envelope and saw that it contained a screenplay, the last thing he needed to deal with at the moment. He found other people's screenplays murderously difficult to read. He put Mahmoud's envelope on a shelf in the kitchen, as far from his desk as possible, and began to work. But soon his curiosity got the best of him. He decided to glance at a few pages.

To his horror, he quickly became intrigued. The story was that of a blind young woman who is brutally raped in Canarsie. She virtually feels her way across the country in pursuit of her assailant, eventually confronting him in the far-off Pacific Northwest. Though crudely organized and unnecessarily weighted down with desert parables, the scenes flew by with a rough fury. There were at least a dozen surprises along the way. The whole of it culminated in a courtroom scene that was both witty and riveting. Major roles existed for both male and female stars. In short, the piece contained all of the dramatic ingredients that Kleiner had resisted in his own work for fear of being thought unsophisticated and losing his puny cult following.

How had the Arab been able to come up with such brilliant work?

The only explanation was that Mahmoud had attended an unheralded film course in the Jewish school that he kept yammering on about—one that, for all Kleiner knew, was secretly funded by Steven Spielberg.

Kleiner was tempted to return the script to Mahmoud, telling him he was wasting his time. But he couldn't bear to have it said of him that he stood in the way of art. Unmistakably, and infuriatingly, this was a work of art.

Kleiner bit the bullet. He included the screenplay in his FedEx package, suggesting that if Himmel had a spare moment, it might be of some small interest.

Later in the day, Kleiner called Naomi Glickstein and got through to her without difficulty. The two arranged to meet at a bar of Kleiner's choosing in the Gramercy Park area, one that was not only convenient but also a magnet for beautiful young fashion models. Kleiner had once dated such a person, who maintained that all models were dumb—with the exception of her.

Before he left, Kleiner made sure that Mahmoud was propped up comfortably in front of the TV set and provided with a delicious portion of eggplant Parmigiana and garlic bread. He'd ordered it from a new restaurant on the ground floor of the building—a real find.

Kleiner left the number of the bar with Mahmoud, in case anything should come up.

"I'll be fine," Mahmoud assured him. "I don't mind at all being left alone in a strange building."

When he arrived at the bar, Naomi was waiting for him in a booth, her face soulful in the candlelight. She wore a loose-fitting jogging suit in place of her standard career-woman out-fit. Unless he was mistaken, there was no bra in the picture. Quickly he brought her up to date on his activities, with special emphasis on his success in spiriting Mahmoud out of Israel.

"Right now, he's watching *Honeymooner* reruns in my apartment."

"Mazel tov," said Naomi, leaning across the table to pinch his cheeks. "You're some humanistic guy."

Kleiner listened with disappointment as she told him that Sol was back in her life, having divorced his wife, given up his practice, and bought a luxury boat for a round-the-world cruise.

"He's asked me to come along," said Naomi. "It would be strictly platonic, with no obligation on my part except to give him regular prostate massages in his cabin. What do you think?"

Not wanting to be guilty of sour grapes, Kleiner took his time in answering.

"I don't know," he said tentatively. "It might be bad for your self-esteem."

"My sentiments exactly," said Naomi. "I can't believe we're on the same wavelength."

The mention of Sol reminded her that the famed urologist was scheduled to appear on a television show that night, one she preferred not to miss.

"I'm anxious to see how he comes across on cable."

"We'll just have one drink," said Kleiner, summoning the waitress.

As he did so, he took a quick look at the cluster of models at the bar, one of whom looked familiar. Contrary to what his model friend had led him to believe, she gave off an air of worldliness and intelligence. A bit later, he excused himself and got up to say hello to her.

"Why don't we pay the check," said Naomi, grabbing his crotch and pulling him back down. "My apartment is just around the corner."

Kleiner paid and they left the restaurant, Naomi still holding on to his crotch as she led him through the streets of

Gramercy Park. Passersby took little notice of the odd arrangement, leading Kleiner to conclude that it was a neighborhood style.

Naomi's apartment was fresh and scrubbed, cheerfully furnished, and had a deco look to it. Flowered pillows were thrown about. There was a Chagall print on the wall. A handsomely carved menorah had a shelf to itself, along with Sabbath candles. Between two bookends were fresh copies of best-selling novels.

"What a nice place," said Kleiner, wondering if two people could live in the apartment comfortably.

"Thank you," said Naomi, turning on the TV. "What I like most is that it's easy to clean."

They had arrived in time to catch Sol summing up his thesis for an audience of troubled males. A distinguished-looking man with a full head of salt-and-pepper hair, he told them not to be concerned about their penises.

"It doesn't matter if it's a little bit of a thing," he said, reassuringly. "A nothing. The main point is that it's *yours*. I'd advise you to go with it and have fun—it's the only game in town."

The applause was vigorous. Naomi turned off the set.

"I thought he came off well," said Kleiner.

"Oh, sure," she said dismissively. "But you should hear him complain about his own *schvonce*."

Despite its scholarly nature, the talk of penises was tremendously arousing to Kleiner. It appeared to have an affect on Naomi as well.

Without preamble, they tore off each other's clothing, Kleiner diving between her long white legs. Unless it was his imagination, she tasted a little Jewish, which is not to say that it was in the area of potato latkes or, for example, a matzoh brei.

Easing him aside, Naomi took his hand with childlike delight and led him into her bedroom, as if he were a lost boy she'd found in the forest.

As she made a place for him on the four-poster bed, Kleiner marveled at the great balance wheel of life that offered him such delights while at the same time denying him choice directing assignments.

Taking a position above him, Naomi swept back her hair and lowered her upper body slowly.

"Go ahead," she said. "Don't be embarrassed. Nosh."

Kleiner lost himself in her great pillowy breasts. But after a time, he sensed that she was distracted.

"Excuse me for one second," she said, then walked across the room, stopping only once to look back at him coquettishly and to give her ass a little shake.

My God, he thought, a Jewish girl, and she shakes her *toches* like a hooker.

After rummaging around in a clothing closet, she emerged with an armful of wired gadgets and contraptions. Carrying them back to the bed, she positioned herself on all fours and attached them to her private parts. The she threw a switch and began to buck and tremble as if she were astride a wild horse.

Kleiner looked on with obvious interest, wondering where he fit into the strange tableau. After a time, she signaled to him. With some difficulty he found a place for himself. Then, to the best of his knowledge, he made love to her—or at least to the arrangement in general.

Clawing at his neck, she glued her hips to his and cried out "*Oy, gevalt!*" then threw another switch and sank back, damp and exhausted.

"You know what that was?" she asked, fanning her giant bosom.

"What's that?"

"A *mecheieh*. And I thank you for it."

Feeling his contribution had been minimal, Kleiner gestured in a sportsmanlike manner toward the technical display.

"Why thank me?"

"Because you made me feel like a woman. And if you're ever a little lonely, don't hesitate to call and I'll be over there like a shot."

In his bachelor days, which more or less included the present, Kleiner had paid little attention to the religious affiliation of the women he dated. The fact that it was a woman was enough. But in the case of the Yiddish-speaking Naomi, there was no question that she was resoundingly Jewish, the only such woman he had been close to as an adult. As he left Naomi's apartment, he wondered if her complex and full-throated sexuality was perhaps representative of the new Jewish woman. The synagogue-goers of his childhood had all seemed models of propriety. The cliché—and as far as he knew, the reality—was that you went elsewhere for all but the most sedate encounters.

Now he had to rethink his position and consider that perhaps it was the Jewish woman, of all people, who was leading the way to a new erotic frontier.

Thinking ahead, he wondered if Naomi would shed her contraptions one by one as they got to know each other, until they came together one day, gadget-free. Or would she continue to add on new devices? Either prospect was fine with Kleiner. He picked up the next day's newspapers at a Pakistani newsstand—a favorite treat—and thought about Naomi's proposal that she visit him on one of his lonely nights. He hurried home to make sure there was an electrical outlet next to his bed.

Fresh and sparkling in their tuxedos, Mahmoud and Kleiner took a cab out to Queens the next day and located the wedding site in an open field in the LeFrak City area. As they mingled with the guests, it quickly became apparent that the bride had not yet shown up, which was causing consternation on both sides of the family.

It was easy for Kleiner to pick out the groom, a taller version of Mahmoud, with features more delicate than those of his older brother. (Since Kleiner, of course, had smashed the older man's nose, he took full responsibility for the disparity in their looks.)

With open arms and a wide grin, Mahmoud ran forward to embrace his only sibling.

"Kamal," he said. "It's me, Mahmoud."

"What are you doing here?" asked Kamal.

"What am I *doing* here?" said Mahmoud with disbelief. "I'm your brother. It's your wedding. How can you ask such a question? I came all the way from Jerusalem, with the kind assistance of Mr. Kleiner, a Jew."

Kleiner felt it was important to point out that his religious affiliation was not an issue.

"Even if I wasn't a Jew, I would have helped."

"I'm sure you would have," said Kamal, giving Kleiner a tight smile. "But it wasn't necessary."

"All right then, I'll go home," said Mahmoud, turning away. "I can see I'm not wanted. Let's go back to the apartment, Mr. Kleiner. I'm sorry I inconvenienced you."

Kleiner couldn't believe his ears. He thought back to their

turbulent meeting at the King David Hotel, the nine stitches in his forehead, the abortive escape to Egypt and their capture and release by the Israelis—not to mention his enormous debt to Louis Blumenthal.

"Inconvenienced me? You did more than that. And we're not going anywhere. I didn't rearrange my life so that I could almost go to a wedding."

"How can I stay? You saw the way my brother treated me."

"He's upset because he has no one to get married to. You would be too."

"It's the fig stand," Mahmoud said bitterly.

He explained that when they were boys in Ashdod, pretending to be grown-ups, they'd built a crude stall beside the road. A dispute arose as to whose name should be affixed to it. The older brother had prevailed. A sign was posted above the stall that read THE FIGS OF MAHMOUD.

"He's never forgiven me," said the older brother.

"Now I understand," said Kleiner. "But we're staying here anyway."

Half an hour later, the bride was still nowhere to be found. Leery of the local police, the groom's family arranged for the wedding guests to split up into teams, which were to fan out across the area in search of her. Mahmoud and Kleiner joined an Arab wedding guest from Las Vegas who informed them that the engaged couple were both investment bankers.

"What brought them together was a shared interest in leveraged buyouts and bat guano."

Taking this as a clue, the trio tracked the bride-to-be down to a small street-side brokerage house. They found her sitting in a makeshift chair, her wedding gown bunched up at her knees, eyes glued to the ticker tape.

"The market's gone through the roof," she said when she saw them. "Isn't it wonderful?"

"What about your wedding?" the Vegas man asked sternly.

"Oh my God," she said, throwing her head back and laughing hysterically. "I forgot all about it."

As the group headed back to the wedding site, Mahmoud introduced himself to the stocky, good-natured bride-to-be and said he'd come all the way from Jerusalem for the festivities.

"That's wonderful," she said.

"Mr. Kleiner here pulled strings to help me."

"That's wonderful too."

Mahmoud turned toward Kleiner.

"I don't like her," he whispered. "She thinks everything is wonderful."

"Clearly she had a happy childhood."

"So did I," said Mahmoud. "But does that mean that everything is wonderful?"

"Chalk it up to nerves," said Kleiner. "Besides, you're not marrying her."

"Still, it's my brother, who still loves me, even though he's being a little standoffish."

The planned union turned out to be a mixed one, which appeared to surprise members of both families. When a rabbi turned up to officiate, at least a dozen relatives keeled over in a dead faint and had to be carried from the premises.

Mahmoud too showed concern.

"This means my brother will become a Jew and I'll lose him forever."

"Do you have him now?" said Kleiner. "Besides, I'm a Jew and look at the bond between us."

"That's true," Mahmoud conceded. "But you don't know my brother. He goes at life whole-hog."

The rabbi was a young man with a reddish beard. His style, perhaps deliberately, was pastoral and non-incendiary.

"May this marriage grow," was his wish, "like vines on a heavenly cottage."

Kleiner admired his gentle style. He felt that if he'd encountered such a man when he was younger, he would currently be more of a full-fledged Jew.

The couple embraced at the end of the ceremony.

"We're going to have such fun," said the bride.

"Wonderful," said the groom, who had evidently picked up her verbal style.

Beneath a canopy, non-denominational hors d'oeuvres were served, the two families keeping a discreet and guarded distance from one another. An exception was the Arab from Vegas. He recognized a Jew he'd served with in the army and approached him.

"How's your foot?" he asked Shep Goldman, who'd caught a piece of shrapnel at Anzio.

"Aches like a sonofabitch."

"But you can still get it up?" asked the Arab with a wink.

"I can't get it down."

The two men gave each other bear hugs, exchanged lascivious comments about the bridesmaids, and pledged to get together in Manhattan.

Sheepishly, Mahmoud approached his brother and handed him the wedding gift he'd selected at F.A.O. Schwarz.

"Aren't you going to open it?" he asked his brother, who was about to toss it on a pile.

"All right, all right," said Kamal, unwrapping the gift, which turned out to be a classic reproduction of a pterodactyl they'd constructed together as boys in the souk.

Begrudgingly, Kamal shook his brother's hand.

"Thank you," he said, then turned to greet some late-arriving well-wishers.

"Give him a hug," said Kleiner to Mahmoud.

"Let him hug me."

"What's the difference," said Kleiner with impatience. He pushed Mahmoud into his brother's arms.

The two men embraced fervently.

"I love you," said Mahmoud, with tears in his eyes.

"I love you too," Kamal said, fighting back his own tears. "I'd ask you to stay with me and Lana while you're here, but we're cramped for space."

"That's all right," said Mahmoud. "It's the thought that counts."

At that point, the band struck up a spirited show tune and a small contingent on the bride's side broke into a grim hora. Across the room, several buxom aunts, related to the groom, began a belly dance, as if in opposition. Amazingly then, the two groups began to mingle. The result was a belly-dancing hora.

Kleiner looked on with satisfaction, pleased that in the teeth of adversity, he had accomplished his goal of bringing the brothers together in the heart of Queens.

"I guess you'll be on your way now," said Kleiner.

"Not just yet," said Mahmoud. "I wouldn't dream of missing your birthday."

The occasion meant little to Kleiner, or at least that's what he pretended. Normally, he let his birthdays come and go. He would have forgotten the one that was imminent if the young Arab (who had obviously discovered the date in his personal papers) hadn't reminded him it was just around the corner.

The last person to celebrate the event with fanfare had been his poor estranged wife. Typically, she'd gone overboard, ordering a truckload of presents, which it took him a year to pay for.

The thought crossed his mind that he could celebrate by inviting Naomi Glickstein to a charming little French restaurant. (Was there any other kind?) But when he acted on the impulse, he found her to be distant and somewhat aloof.

"I don't know," she said in a weak voice. "Frankly, I'm a little *fartutst* at the moment."

"Maybe this will get you out of it. Suppose I take a rain check."

"We'll see," said Naomi vaguely.

Kleiner was disappointed. He theorized that perhaps she was embarrassed because he knew about her reliance on complex gadgetry for sexual release. Or possibly her former urologist lover was putting pressure on her. In any case, he was happy to have an Arab and a dog for company.

In the several days that followed, Mahmoud made mysterious trips about the city on his own. He reported only that he had priced lutes, visited the Chrysler Building, and toured the offices of the *Village Voice*.

With little to occupy himself until he heard from Himmel about the location shots, Kleiner killed time in the library, comparing the movie dialogue of Joe Mankiewicz and F. Scott Fitzgerald to see which was superior. (The novelist's dialogue was elevated, too much of a mouthful for the screen. It was better suited to the page.) He spent the actual day of his birthday in a Village art house watching *She*, a favorite film, and one he'd sat through thirty times as a boy. Then he treated himself to a foot-long hot dog; for contrast, he bought swordfish steak for his dinner with Mahmoud, also a box of Flavor Snacks for the dog, if indeed that's what it was.

As a final treat, he bought a new true-crimer at the bookstore, one in which a golden-haired and outwardly happy couple turns out to be sitting on a time bomb of incest, infidelity, and insurance fraud—all of it culminating in the ax murder of the husband's car-hop mistress. Before making the purchase, he checked the black-and-white photos that were inserted in the book to make sure the doomed couple was golden-haired and attractive enough to sustain his interest.

When he returned to his apartment, he found there was a party in full swing. The living room was filled with unwanted guests and a smiling Mahmoud in a velveteen jacket, acting as their host.

Though it was no doubt unintended, the Arab, astonishingly, had gathered together in a single room every person in the city that Kleiner hated—or at least had given him trouble of some kind.

Among the merry-makers was Henry Darlington, a black man who had posed as Kleiner and used his Visa card to pay for a three-week stay in a private room at Lenox Hill Hospital; Georgina Gray, a fashion model who had swept out of a cabin without explanation while they were halfway along in making love on Shelter Island; Louis Blumenthal, no doubt there to collect the enormous debt Kleiner owed him; and Gabe Ginns, an acquaintance of twenty-five years who had invited him to dinner at a steakhouse one Christmas Eve to announce, after dessert, that he was ending their friendship.

"I'm just not getting enough out of it," he'd said, leaving Kleiner with the check.

The only guest who didn't immediately represent trouble was the Yiddish-speaking Naomi Glickstein. Still, when Kleiner greeted her, even she looked at him with eyes that were hooded with suspicion.

How Mahmoud had been able to put together the swinish group on such short notice was beyond Kleiner. Additionally, the Arab had ordered hors d'oeuvres from a trendy restaurant that Kleiner no longer frequented; he'd had a shouting match with the owner over a blatantly padded check.

Clenching his teeth, Kleiner thanked the group generally for being there, then went upstairs to put on his good sports jacket. When he returned, he poured himself a drink of the off-brand Scotch that Mahmoud had supplied, one Kleiner wouldn't serve to his worst enemies—several of whom were there. Then he took a bite of a watery crabmeat canapé, looked at the grim faces in the room, and prepared for the worst evening of his life.

Mahmoud put on some bossa nova music and adjusted the harsh lighting so that it became warm and ingratiating. Remarkably, Kleiner's spirits began to lift a bit. His bitter reaction upon entering the room must have been apparent at first, with the result that the guests kept their distance. But then Henry Darlington, who'd apparently lost his hair during the fraudulent hospital stay, approached Kleiner, kissed him on the forehead, and handed him a stack of worn currency.

"I can't thank you enough for your kindness, my brother."

"Not at all," said Kleiner.

He took a quick look at the money that had been handed to him and calculated that there was more than enough to cover the old Visa bill he'd been forced to settle. Suddenly, he recalled that Darlington lived on the fringes of life. He had to do everything from light bodyguard work to the delivery of milk during labor disputes in order to survive. There was also a rumor that he traded in hot Torahs.

"Are you sure you can spare it?" asked Kleiner as he pocketed the money.

"Not really," said Darlington, "but there are some extra twenties in there by way of interest."

Throwing his mouth open in a wide soundless laugh, he headed for the bar.

Next to approach Kleiner was the towering model, Georgina Gray. With close-cropped hair and a cigarette hanging from her lips, she'd kept her downtown look but gained some weight, a change that Kleiner found appealing.

"I want to apologize," she said. "I had a conflict between that stupid modeling thing in Milano and the career I'd always sought in television infotainment. I suppose it all came together while we were making love on Shelter Island. No doubt you blamed my sudden departure on your performance in bed. I can assure you that wasn't the case at all. In any event, I've left modeling and become a sous chef, which has made me much happier.

"And don't worry," she said, pinching his ass. "I owe you half a fuck."

Kleiner was tempted to ask waggishly, "Which half?" but he was able to rein himself in.

His spirits rising, he joined Mahmoud, who was in whispered colloquy with Naomi Glickstein.

"Are you having a good time, Mr. Kleiner?" asked Mahmoud.

"Not bad," said Kleiner, who wondered about the subject of their intense discussion.

"I'm glad," said Mahmoud. "I went to great lengths to make sure that this would be the happiest birthday of your life."

"And you succeeded," said Kleiner, wondering why he was sparing the Arab's feelings.

Then he turned to Naomi, who continued to be in a dark mood.

He was about to ask if she was all right when he heard a weak voice behind him.

"I'm dying."

Whirling around, he saw that the dire words had been spoken by Gabe Ginns, the college roommate who had abruptly ended their friendship after twenty-five years.

"I'm sorry to hear that," said Kleiner, though he saw no sign of ill health in the stocky, ruddy-cheeked Bostonian.

"It's not definite," said Ginns. "They promised to let me know. But I thought you might feel better if you patched things up."

"*You* dropped *me*," said Kleiner.

"All right, forget it," said Ginns. "You've always been a selfish bastard and you still are."

Turning, he headed for the door.

"Wait a minute," said Kleiner, catching his arm. "Don't leave on that note. I'm sorry for what I did, even though I don't know what it is."

At this, his friend broke into a yellow smile.

"I love you, you sonofabitch," said Ginns, throwing his arms around Kleiner. "Are you going to serve any food?"

"It's up to him," said Kleiner, nodding toward Mahmoud.

Ginns was a Boston Brahmin who on occasion affected a street style.

"I've been checking him out. He's got his head up his ass. No food, no broads, no atmosphere. Get rid of him," said Ginns, walking off abruptly.

Now that he'd repaired his friendship with the mercurial Ginns, Kleiner wondered if he wasn't better off without it.

As he mulled this over, he was alarmed to see Louis Blumenthal bearing down upon him.

"Nice party," said Blumenthal, taking a sip of his enormous drink.

"Thank you," said Kleiner, steeling himself for the huge favor he was sure he'd be asked.

"Things work out in Jerusalem?" asked Blumenthal, ominously holding his glass in front of his face and staring out over the rim.

"Fine," said Kleiner guardedly.

Blumenthal stirred his drink with a little finger.

"There's something you might be able to help me out with."

"Name it," said Kleiner, praying that whatever it was wouldn't make him miserable for the rest of his life.

"My wife is fainting to go to the Academy Awards. You know everybody out there. Can you set up a pair of tickets?"

Kleiner almost collapsed with relief. He belonged to the Academy and got tickets every year, which he threw away, not out of disrespect but for shame at not being a nominee.

Nonetheless, he fell back as if in shock.

"That's a big one, Louis."

"I know, I know . . . but it would mean a lot to me. She's driving me crazy and I don't know where to turn."

"Let me work on it."

"Thanks," said Blumenthal. "And incidentally, that kid you brought over from Israel is sensational. Where did he learn so much about Fats Waller?"

"Probably at Jewish school."

"Figures," said Blumenthal with an ironic chuckle.

Kleiner felt tremendously lighter, prepared now to enjoy fully his party—the best, when he thought about it, that he'd ever had.

Tapping his glass, Mahmoud called the group to attention and proposed a toast.

"To Mr. Kleiner, who got me out of Jerusalem so that I could attend my brother's wedding, even though I'm a despised Arab. Health, happiness, and may he finally get a good job.

"*Le chaim.*"

"*Le chaim*," the group cried out as one.

Kleiner, who wasn't good at speeches, kept his remarks short.

"Thank you, everyone. I didn't know I was going to have a good time, but I am."

"Nicely phrased," said Darlington.

All in the room drank deeply.

At that point, the phone rang. Mahmoud, who seemed to know in advance who the caller was, picked up the receiver and handed it to Kleiner.

"Hi, sweet," said Kleiner's estranged wife, her voice husky and appealing and giving no indication that they hadn't seen each other for two years. Suddenly he wanted the two years back.

"Emma . . . where are you?"

"In Miami. . . .Your friend called and said he was giving you a party. I wanted to wish you the best."

"I'm glad you did. Do you like it there?"

"You'd love it."

"But do *you* like it?"

"I like it too. Would you like to talk to Becky?"

"Just tell her hello," said Kleiner.

When they'd first met, his stepdaughter had thrown potato salad in his face. He feared she might try it again from twelve hundred miles away.

"We both love you," said Emma. "Have a great time and make sure to give yourself hugs and kisses."

"I love you too," said Kleiner, putting down the receiver.

The call both pleased Kleiner and threw him off stride. When he left Emma, she'd been frail and unable to cope with her various addictions. Now she seemed robust and healthy and he longed to be with her. He thought about a reunion with her. But maybe she'd be addicted to reunions. As the group sang "Happy Birthday," he pulled out her driver's license photo, which he still kept in his wallet, and stared at her pretty Seattle face. Then the door flew open and one of Himmel's crews came in and began to gather up the furniture.

"Put that down," said Mahmoud as the foreman lifted one end of a couch. "Don't you realize it's Mr. Kleiner's birthday?"

When the foreman ignored him, the Arab jumped on the man and tore off his tank top. A fight broke out; all joined in with the exception of Naomi Glickstein, who stood in a corner, arms folded, as if she were protecting her large breasts. At the center of the melee, Mahmoud flailed about at first as if he were an enraged drag queen. Then he switched to a surprisingly polished boxing style, reminiscent of the late, great Kid Gavilán.

Kleiner tried to restore order, but the commotion roused the neighbors, bringing the UN man to the door in his nightgown, the pet monkey on his shoulder.

"Can someone explain this gross behavior?" he asked.

Before anyone could answer, Mahmoud's dog, or whatever it was, flew out of nowhere and tore at the monkey's throat, killing it in an instant.

Kneeling beside his lifeless pet, the stunned UN man began to sob deeply.

"Klaus is dead," he said to Kleiner. "You have broken my heart. And you're not even in the building legally."

The police arrived soon after. Quickly they established that Mahmoud had been the instigator, arresting him on the spot.

"I'll go with him," said Kleiner as the Arab was led off in handcuffs.

"That's against regulations," said one of the officers. "But you're welcome to come to the arraignment."

Kleiner was so law-abiding that he didn't even know what an arraignment was. But he knew it wasn't good.

The crew decided to call off the shoot and left, followed by Kleiner's guests, who filed out in silence.

Gabe Ginns was the exception.

"Hold your head up. You just gave one of the great fucking parties of our time.

"I'll let you know about my tests."

Alone in the apartment, Kleiner felt awful about having to desert Mahmoud. The Arab had given him a fabulous party— up to a point—and had only been trying to protect his furniture.

Though the hour was late, Kleiner called his attorney in Connecticut, aware that Rizzoli liked to work behind the scenes and had a fear of appearing in court.

After listening to Kleiner's story, Rizzoli was true to form in his response.

"I'd let it run its course."

This was advice he had given to Kleiner many times. Once in a while it was sound.

Kleiner put the swordfish in the freezer, swept up the living room, and cautiously fed the killer dog.

Then he tried to get some sleep. When this proved to be impossible, he called Central Booking and was told by the arresting officer that Mahmoud had been arraigned and was being taken to Rikers Island.

"And the bail?" asked Kleiner, pretending he knew something about the law.

"Don't even ask. As a visiting Arab, your friend falls into a high-risk category of being likely to flee. The figure is out of sight."

Kleiner didn't dare ask the amount.

"How's he feeling?"

"I don't get into that."

He hung up. Kleiner thought of his poor friend among thieves and rapists. He was sorry he hadn't left him in the Arab Quarter, where he would have been better off, even though the area had troubles of its own.

To distract himself, he put his Academy Award tickets in an envelope. He was about to go downstairs and mail them to Louis Blumenthal when he heard the humming of the fax machine, his only item of contemporary equipment.

Tearing off the communication, he read the following:

To: Kleiner
From: Naomi Joan Glickstein

> You lied, Kleiner. There was no reason
> To lie, yet you did anyway. Told a lie.
> Why did you lie, Kleiner? Does lying come easy
> To you? My guess is that it does. So you just
> Went ahead and lied, lied, lied. I could burst
> From how you lied.
> Sincerely,
> Naomi Joan Glickstein

There was no question that the repetition of the word "lie" was effective as a rhetorical device. But it was devastating to Kleiner, who considered himself to be a somewhat honorable man. Each "lie" was like an arrow in his chest. Also, he was puzzled as to the nature of what he had lied about. To clear up the confusion, he fired off his own fax.

> Dear Naomi,
> I just received your message and I thank you for it. But just out of curiosity, what did I lie about?
> With continuing affection,
> William Kleiner

Her reply came back minutes later:

> Don't bullshit me. You said you were single. In my world, that's a lie.

Kleiner read her latest communication and was relieved that there was only one "lie" in it. He wondered if indeed her accusation had some validity. Yet he couldn't remember any discussion of his marital status. Possibly he had been a little vague about it, but obviously this was a sore point with Naomi, who had been freshly betrayed by her urologist lover. He wondered if it was possible to patch things up—oh, those tits—although obviously this was a poor time to try.

Kleiner's producer arrived the next morning, having just come in from Los Angeles on the red-eye.

A man of roughly Kleiner's age, Himmel had dyed his hair so that it was henna-colored and had his teeth re-enameled to make him more appealing to actresses. Though his personal life was troubled, he owned vast properties in Central America and had amassed the world's largest collection of stun guns.

Sailing into the apartment, the first thing he did was

check the air conditioners, which had obsessed him from the moment Kleiner moved in.

"Weren't you supposed to pay me for these?" he asked, running his finger along one of them.

"I thought it was part of the deal," said Kleiner, who was in no position to shell out thousands for used appliances.

"No way," said Himmel, sinking into a designer chair. "But listen, don't worry about the Arab. I got the studio to drop the charges and he'll be out of Rikers this afternoon. And I *love* his script. Absolutely love it. I could fuck that script I love it so much. Does he want to direct?"

"I didn't ask him," said Kleiner, who was less than thrilled by the producer's excitement. "What did you think of my location shots?"

"They're a little too Jewish," said Himmel. "I know, I know, it's Israel, but still. Anyway, I don't want to talk about that. I can *make* this kid's movie. Has anyone else seen the script?"

"It seems unlikely. He just got in from Jerusalem."

"Good," said Himmel.

Then he lowered his eyes as if it was painful to get his next words out.

"By the way, the guy down the hall complained to the board. I'm gonna have to ask you to leave."

"Because of the monkey?" said Kleiner. "It wasn't my dog. I'm not even sure it's a dog."

"That's not it," said Himmel. "I got the studio to send him another monkey. The kid can stay—but they want you out of here."

As soon as Himmel left, Kleiner went downstairs and got some empty cartons from the liquor store. Then he returned to the apartment and—as he had done so many times before—began to pack the books and papers he knew in his heart he really didn't need. Only this time around, he was filled with bitterness. He couldn't believe that an Arab he'd helped so graciously had turned on him by not only getting a movie deal but also inheriting his apartment. He was sorry he had disrupted his life to see to it that Mahmoud got to his brother's wedding. Kleiner made a vow. From that point on, when it came to the Israeli Arab question, he would take a hardline position.

Later in the day, Mahmoud returned, wearing Ray-Bans and a soft leather jacket that made him look like a director. Kleiner dutifully told him about the script's joyous reception and that for the time being the apartment was his.

"But that's out of the question," said Mahmoud. "With your permission, I'll fight with all my heart to get you involved as an assistant director. Or maybe as one of the many executive producers."

"That won't be necessary."

"As for the apartment, there's no reason why you can't continue to live in an alcove upstairs while Naomi and I work in the living room."

Naomi. Suddenly, Kleiner saw it all clearly. While Mahmoud was supposedly pricing lutes and visiting historical landmarks, he'd sought out Naomi and told her Kleiner was a married man. Then the two had begun an affair. No wonder she had looked at him with such distrust at his birthday party. The call from his wife, cleverly arranged by the Arab, had cinched it.

"Congratulations," said Kleiner, who hated sarcasm, except when he was the one who was using it. "I hope the two of you are very happy."

Kleiner arranged to have his cartons picked up and stored; then he walked across town and checked into a dreary hotel that matched his mood. The desk clerk told him that Charles Bukowski had spent a weekend on the fourth floor. Still, he was unable to shake his depression. It was only when he realized that he had no job, no prospects, very little money, and had just lost his apartment and a hot-looking girlfriend that he understood the reason for it and began to feel better. A bright spot was that he no longer had to duck in and out of his apartment like a criminal, pretending the spacious duplex was his. Even in the bleak hotel room, where the pipes kept him up all night, he was actually registered. If someone wanted to find him, all they had to do was ask the hotel clerk, who would put them through to Room 115, the temporary residence of William Kleiner. And, of course, he no longer had to concern himself with the fortunes of a treacherous Arab.

Feeling light and free, Kleiner checked out of the hotel, took his car out of the garage, and headed for the open road.

PART THREE

Kleiner told a friend, who knew Emma, that he was angry at her—the pills, the vodka bottles. The friend said, "You should get down on your knees and thank God you have such a woman in your life."

Kleiner, not a good listener, heard this.

As he left the city, Kleiner was aware that he was part of an American tradition—striking out across the vast frontier in search of adventure and renewal. The night before, in the same bold spirit that had forged a mighty nation, he had closed his eyes and thrown a dart at the map, determined to journey to whatever city the fates selected. When it landed on Cincinnati, he took it out and stuck it in Miami Beach. As long as he was seeking adventure, he might as well do it in warm weather.

The selection of Miami was not entirely arbitrary. Emma lived there, of course, but he had been taken there as a boy and had seen pictures of himself sitting on a pink flamingo made of stone. He was determined to find that flamingo and sit on it once again. That would give closure to the whole flamingo thing, although how it would help him earn a living wasn't clear.

Driving day and night, he stopped only in Georgia, where there was a statue of the nation's first screenwriter, who had done a first draft and a polish in Savannah. Had the picture gotten a green light? If so, there was no mention of it. Kleiner was determined to stay in the hospitable city and possibly go no farther, but when a group of teenagers refused to let him into a playground game of hoops, he decided to push on.

In Miami, he checked into a small hotel in South Beach whose clientele was made up of only Jews and Jamaicans—although there was no evidence of a restrictive policy on the part of the management. After catching a little sun, he called Emma. She seemed out of breath and harassed, but agreed to meet him later in the day for lunch.

They sat outside at the crowded News Café. She looked fresh and slim; he noticed that the freckles were back on her perfect nose. His heart jumped, just as it had when he'd first met her at a Lillian Gish tribute. At the time, she had only a few addictions.

Not quite scolding him, she suggested it was unfair of Kleiner to show up after two years as if nothing had changed.

"What if I had a lover?"

"Do you?" he asked, strangely—and unfairly—panicked.

"Not particularly, but what if I did?"

The possibility was chilling. Kleiner agreed that he was asking for a great deal.

"I'm tempted to wine and dine you and shower you with gifts and gradually insinuate myself back into your affections."

"That's not a bad little idea."

Kleiner, of course, had done that already—when they first met—and he wasn't anxious to repeat himself. Nonetheless, wearily, in the weeks that followed, he took her to dozens of restaurants, danced with her in nightclubs, and arranged to have a huge carton of white jellybeans poured into the window of her condo. Digging into the last of his pension funds, he hired a plane to fly over, trailing a banner that said I LOVE YOU. Then he flew one of her sisters in from rural Tennessee for a weekend reunion. As it turned out, it was the wrong sister—

one that she hated—but Emma appreciated the thought and invited him to move back in with her.

"I can't keep eating in all those restaurants," she said. "And I'm missing *Saturday Night Live*."

Though the invitation was lukewarm, Kleiner snatched at it like a drowning man, insisting that he take the couch while she kept the bed.

Thus he began a new life with his old family.

With no directing assignment on the horizon, Kleiner broadened himself by touring South Beach, talking to ship-jumpers from Palumbo, Jewish cops with Magnums on their hips, and German students who apologized for Munich's skin-heads but scolded him for *Exxon Valdez*. He enjoyed the ano-nymity of the beach, where a new Cuban friend, for example, would have no idea that he was unemployed in the film busi-ness. And on Arthur Godfrey Drive, he felt he could be as Jewish as he wanted to be, even more so than in Israel. On one occasion he shouted out, "*Farblondget*," at the top of his lungs and caused only a minor commotion.

By day, Emma worked at the Cluebox, a store she had opened that catered to lovers of genteel English mysteries, thus putting the last of her addictions to profitable use. The store did a surprisingly brisk business, with models on skateboards drifting in to browse, and gay body-builders taking the latest Julian Symons off to read at tanning salons. The only employee was a savagely handsome black-haired man named Diarmid, a pipe smoker who wore a shawl and scowled at customers, with no appreciable effect on sales. Kleiner sensed that he was the lover Emma had hinted at, but in his new maturity, he refused to ask if this were true—not that he wasn't dying to know.

At night, they had dinner at Emma's condo with Kleiner's stepdaughter. Becky had become great-eyed and willowy, an enchanted child, no longer disposed to throw potato salad in his face.

"Are we Jewish?" she asked one night.

"I am," said Kleiner. "Your mother's not."

"I've given it a great deal of thought and I've decided I'd like to be a Jewish sportscaster."

With deference, Kleiner looked over at his wife.

"At least she wants to be *something*," said Emma encouragingly.

Even when the skies were overcast, Kleiner felt he was in paradise. One day a black cloud appeared in the form of an announcement in the *Miami Herald*. The director Mahmoud Salah planned to shoot the opening scenes of his new movie in South Beach. At the moment he was looking for extras.

Across the breakfast table, Emma saw Kleiner's face fall. He then told her of his troubled history with the opportunistic Arab.

"The announcement has nothing to do with you," she said supportively.

Becky took his face in her hands and pressed her forehead against his.

"Just ignore him."

But this was a difficult assignment for Kleiner. The Arab's triumphant appearance in Miami reminded him of his own lowly position in the entertainment industry, if indeed he even had one. Was there no place on Earth where he was safe from Mahmoud and the fucking movie business?

Soon afterward, miraculously, Kleiner ran into an old friend named Vogel, a former press agent who now ran a failing Spanish restaurant in Coconut Grove. The restaurant included a small cabaret; it was Vogel's idea to stimulate his dinner trade by putting on a transvestite version of *Uncle Vanya*.

"Would you consider directing?"

Though Kleiner had never worked with trannies, he jumped at the chance and told Vogel to count him in.

Immediately he set about finding talented performers for the key roles, taking Becky along to the auditions. At the end of the first day, she announced that she wanted to do what he did.

"I don't actually do anything," said Kleiner.

"I don't care. I want to do it too. Is math helpful?"

"Absolutely."

"That's great. I'm good at math."

Within a short period, Kleiner had assembled his cast. After an initial period of self-consciousness, in which there were a great many Elton John jokes bandied about, the trannies warmed to the tricky Chekhovian roles. The production was soon on its feet.

The opening performance was greeted warmly by the local press. As a result, the restaurant quickly doubled the number of dinners served.

With the play off and running, Kleiner found himself with more time on his hands. Each day he took Becky to ballet school in North Miami. He was enormously proud of her when she landed the coveted role of Clara in *The Nutcracker*. Annoyingly, there was jealousy on the part of other parents. They felt Becky had benefited from Kleiner's position in the entertainment industry—a ridiculous charge, considering he hadn't had a real job in two years.

On weekends, he and Becky searched for the pink flamingo. One day they located the site of the Vane Hotel, which was now nothing more than a pile of rubble. A notice was posted, saying that a wholesale drugstore would soon be erected on the property.

There was no sign of the statue.

"Somebody probably took it home," said Becky.

"I don't think so."

"I'm sure of it. They probably wanted to keep it in their living room and not let anyone else sit on it."

"Are there such people?"

"Of course, Mr. Daddy. Didn't you know that?"

On the day of Becky's ballet recital, Kleiner received a call from Naomi Glickstein.

"You probably don't remember me, but we dated briefly in Jerusalem—and then in the city."

She hesitated a moment, then said, "The bubbies girl that you lied to."

"Of course I remember," said Kleiner. "How are you getting along?"

"Mezzo, mezzo," said Naomi. "We've run into some trouble on the film. The completion bond fell through at the last minute and Mahmoud is taking it badly. He's out on a ledge at the moment, threatening to commit suicide. And he says you're the only one he'll talk to."

"I'm on my way to my daughter's recital."

She let out a sigh. "All right, so he'll jump."

The guilt trip took effect.

"What's the address?" Kleiner asked.

She gave him the number of a high-rise on Collins Avenue, the top section of which had been taken over by the production.

"We're on the eighteenth floor. You'd better come quickly."

After Kleiner hung up, he had to hold on to a chair for support. He was terrified of heights and couldn't even get up on a ladder to change a bulb. The very thought of an Arab, one he knew so well, standing on a ledge, way up in the sky, made him dizzy and nauseous.

He told Emma about the call.

"Fuck him," he said. "After what he's put me through. Let him jump."

"You can't do that. Go over there and see if you can help. I'll save a seat for you at the recital."

"What about my fear of heights?"

"You'll get over it," she said.

And for the moment, he believed her.

Kleiner took a cab to the address he'd been given and had a surprisingly smooth ride up on the elevator.

Clustered around the production office were concerned crew members and half a dozen police officers.

When Naomi saw him, she ran over and gave him a hug.

"Thank God," she said, once again unsettling him with her enormous breasts. Was it his imagination, or did she shift them around enticingly?

She led him out to the terrace, where a police sergeant was conducting what sounded like generic movie dialogue with Mahmoud.

"There is always darkness before the dawn. I don't have to tell you that, Mahmoud. You're no different from millions of others, except that they refuse to take the easy way out. Any coward can splatter himself all over the pavement."

Ten feet away, crouched on a narrow ledge, Mahmoud stared at the horizon with blank eyes and appeared to hear nothing.

Kleiner introduced himself to the sergeant, saying the Arab was an old friend.

"Let me take a crack at him."

"Be my guest," said the sergeant, stepping aside. "I can't budge the fucker."

"Mahmoud," said Kleiner, taking hold of the terrace railing and trying not to faint. "I heard you were in trouble and I thought I'd drop by."

Mahmoud responded in a weak voice.

"Thank you, Mr. Kleiner. I hope it didn't interfere with your schedule."

"Not at all," said Kleiner. "What's the story?"

Mahmoud held his temples, a gesture Kleiner remembered from room service, back at the King David.

"The production fell apart and now I have nothing. The psychology. It's worse on the coast than it is in the souk."

"You'll get another film deal," said Kleiner, drawing a nod of admiration from the police sergeant. No doubt he wondered why he hadn't thought of the same ploy.

"I don't want one," said Mahmoud. "They have no values. They'll raise you to the sky, then when you're of no further use, they'll drop you like a dead fly. I should have listened to you."

Kleiner didn't recall issuing such an advisory to the Arab, but felt it prudent to nod in agreement all the same.

"Now that it's out of your system," he told the Arab, "you can come back in."

"Who said it's out of my system?"

"If I handed you a broom, would you grab the other end and let me pull you over here?"

"No way," said Mahmoud, who had Americanized his speech somewhat.

"I shouldn't even be here," said Kleiner, reversing his psychology. "Not after what you did to me."

"What did I do? You're better off now."

Though it was hardly a time for introspection, Kleiner considered the Arab's comment and saw that there was some truth to it. Yes, he was still unemployed in the film industry. But he had his family back, an apartment he could more or less call his own, a child he adored, and excellent weather. It's true that he had lost the sensuous Naomi Glickstein. But their romance, such as it was, had been based primarily on sex and Yiddish phrases and would probably have worn thin after a couple of great months.

"You have a point," said Kleiner. "Now you can come back in."

"I can't, Mr. Kleiner. Hollywood destroyed me. I'm out of gas."

He stood erectly now. The wind blew back his hair, revealing the bald spot he was always worried about. He wore khaki pants and an old blue windbreaker. Kleiner found this affecting, though why he should be touched by such an innocuous garment was beyond him. He thought of their meeting at the King David, Mahmoud playing bingo with a patient in the Jerusalem clinic, the dinosaur model in his room, the boyish stubble on his face when Kleiner hugged him in the souk and promised that somehow he would deliver him up to Queens.

After a quick peek at the concrete courtyard below, Kleiner stepped out on the ledge, his back against the building. Not taking time to be nauseous, he inched his way toward the Arab and grabbed his hand. Mahmoud pulled one way, Kleiner the other. After a brief tug-of-war, Kleiner gently and stubbornly pulled him back onto the terrace.

"Thank you, Mr. Kleiner," the Arab said simply.

"Don't mention it."

"I know Mahmy," said Naomi, having given him a horrible nickname. She was breathing heavily. "He wasn't fooling around."

"I realize that," said Kleiner, wishing he could have one last shot at her enormous breasts—and trying to damp down the thought.

"Let me come home with you," said Mahmoud. "I'd love to meet your family. Maybe I can stay with you for a while."

"I don't think so," said Kleiner.

"Please, sir. Your wife sounded so nice on the phone. We can all be together."

"Out of the question."

"I promise not to get sexy with Mrs. Kleiner. And I'll teach your daughter to swim in the ocean, far out where nobody goes."

"She knows how to swim. You're on your own now, Mahmoud."

Kleiner looked at his watch and saw that he had little time to get to the recital.

"I'd better get going," he said to Naomi.

"Let me give you a lift."

She was more desirable than ever, but Kleiner recalled her clumsy walking style and cringed at the thought of her behind the wheel.

"I don't want to bother you."

"Please," she said. "It's the least I can do."

In the studio car, Kleiner told her of his infatuation with his stepdaughter.

"You're very lucky," said Naomi. Her driving style was surprisingly smooth. "I'll bet she's gorgeous."

Kleiner detected some sadness in her voice. "You'll have a family too."

"If my two-picture deal at Universal is picked up, maybe. If not, who knows."

"How'd you get the film deal?"

"An executive at the studio went wild over my poem. Maybe you remember it. It's called 'I Could Burst.'"

"How could I forget it?" said Kleiner.

As they pulled up to the community center, he thanked Naomi for the ride. He leaned over and kissed her, aware that he would never see her again.

"*Zei gezunt*, Naomi."

"*Zei gezunt*, sweet princealah."

The ballet had already begun when Kleiner entered the theater. He had missed some of Becky's performance, though fortunately not her solo. Groping his way through the darkness, he found Emma, who had put a coat over his seat.

"What took you so long?"

"There was more to it than I thought."

"Did you get dizzy?"

"No."

"Seeee," she said, patting his knee. "Now, let's be quiet."

Moments later, Becky made her appearance. On her toes, high and delighted, she smiled through braces and danced on skinny, shivering legs, reminiscent of the lost pink flamingo. Far from Jerusalem, Kleiner leaned forward on a rented director's chair and entered the Promised Land.

ABOUT THE AUTHOR

Bruce Jay Friedman lives in New York City. A novelist, short story writer, playwright, memoirist, and screenwriter, he is the author of nineteen books, including *Stern* (1962), *A Mother's Kisses* (1964), *The Lonely Guy's Book of Life* (1978), and *Lucky Bruce: A Literary Memoir* (2011). His best-known works of stage and screen include the off-Broadway hit *Steambath* (1970) and the screenplays for *Stir Crazy* (1980) and *Splash* (1984), the latter of which received an Academy Award nomination. As editor of the anthology *Black Humor* (1965), Friedman helped popularize the distinctive literary style of that name in the United States and is widely regarded as one of its finest practitioners. According to the *New York Times*, his prose is "a pure pleasure machine."

EBOOKS BY BRUCE JAY FRIEDMAN

FROM OPEN ROAD MEDIA

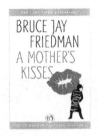 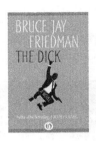 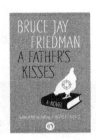

Available wherever ebooks are sold

OPEN ROAD
INTEGRATED MEDIA

Open Road Integrated Media is a digital publisher and multimedia content company. Open Road creates connections between authors and their audiences by marketing its ebooks through a new proprietary online platform, which uses premium video content and social media.

Videos, Archival Documents, and New Releases

Sign up for the Open Road Media newsletter and get news delivered straight to your inbox.

Sign up now at
www.openroadmedia.com/newsletters

FIND OUT MORE AT
WWW.OPENROADMEDIA.COM

FOLLOW US:
@openroadmedia and
Facebook.com/OpenRoadMedia

CPSIA information can be obtained at www.ICGtesting.com
Printed in the USA
BVOW08s1420140915

417692BV00001B/1/P

9 781504 011730